"Since your canvas is smaller than nature (you have to) use a green that's greener than nature. This is the Truth of the Lie."

Paul Gauguin

"Real order carries impurity within itself, destruction."

Italo Calvino

"Builds are selected on a specific artistic deferential. In a sense, they are genetically encouraged toward a replication of the creative achievements of their historic antecedents. But time and circumstance are also a formative factor, without which, their output is less than assured. That is why it is essential they be subject to proper encouragement and care if ever they are to reach the apex of their potential."

(From Carlos Yakamura's shared text solicitation: *The Pro-Creative Beneficence of Modified Diploid Precocity or A Brief Guide to a Long-Term Investment in the Boutique Children of Wiloughby.*)

Lo

A Novel

BRADFORD TATUM

LO: A Novel

For information about this title or to order other books and/or electronic media, contact the publisher:
Soft Moon Press
Los Angeles, California
softmoonpress@gmail.com

ISBN: 978-0-9844896-4-0 (print)
ISBN: 978-0-9844896-5-7 (eBook)

Publisher's Cataloging-In-Publication Data
(Prepared by The Donohue Group, Inc.)

Names: Tatum, Bradford, 1965 March 29- author.
Title: Lo : a novel / Bradford Tatum.
Description: Los Angeles, California : Soft Moon Press, [2022]
Identifiers: ISBN 9780984489640 (print) | ISBN 9780984489657 (ebook)
Subjects: LCSH: Mars (Planet)--Colonies--Fiction. | Space colonies--Fiction. | Rich people--Mars--Fiction. | Fathers and sons--Fiction. | Transgenic organisms--Mars--Fiction. | LCGFT: Science fiction. | Noir fiction. | Thrillers (Fiction)
Classification: LCC PS3620.A893 L6 2022 (print) | LCC PS3620.A893 (ebook) | DDC 813/.6--dc23

For my father

A WINTER ON MARS

Chapter 1

Lo meets Harlem in the Water Builder's yard, not far from the holding tanks, where the hum of the jostling H and O molecules might dim the thundering of their hearts. While they appear as two young people, they are what is known here on Wiloughby as Builds. Which does not mean they are not completely human. It simply means they are someone else's idea of human. They are not used to their bodies being their own. They are not used to acting on a passion their owners did not pay for.

I am a cook and so I think of them as flavors. Licorice and kiwi for her. Something dark and ripened in a cellar for the boy. A perfect combination of opposite essences. They will simmer into the escape from the expected that all cooks aim for.

Harlem puts her hands on him first, the hollows of her palms cupping the knobs of his narrow shoulders. She does this fluidly, in waltz time. She has been selected from the DNA of a long dead and famous Russian dancer, so this is natural for her. Lo stiffens at her caress. He has been constituted from longer dead but equally famous painters, so he is used to only his eyes touching the world. She parts her version of Pavlova's lips. He tastes her breath. Sugared dioxide, something slightly lyrical. There is music in her breath, in the melody inside her and suddenly he is reminded of the reason he has chosen to meet her.

He has come to free her music.

He studies the stalks of her eyelashes, the sea-creature shock of her mouth. He pulls her toward him. Her lips taste pink. What he can imagine as pink while it lives. He is careful not to remove his mouth from hers as his fingers find the mag-buttons of her hemp romper. He is deft at this, having practiced the movements on himself in the dark. He feels her ignite, then shy, but Lo pulls her closer as he imagined he would.

With his lips still pressed to hers and in a gesture no more than a distracted sweep up her torso, he cleaves her neatly from navel to throat with the sharpened edge of his coin. He is careful to apply a bit more pressure at the smooth divot at the base of her throat, knowing the blood will flood her vocal cords and muffle her cry. What scream she has left, he will swallow himself.

Her blood wells hotly as he imagined. Her breath tastes now of secret salt and metal scent. Her eyes wide, chest heaving against the lie of the air that eludes her, Lo recognizes her colors now.

Turner's grand storms.

Rothko's citrusy gradients.

These are not the artists whose genes motivate his own brush, he notices. Just two that he admires. He is made of John Singer-Sargent and Masaccio, two academic realists with centuries between them.

Lo charts the way she stops. He waits until she is still, until her wound begins to congeal a shiny black, frustrated, then mournful that her bright, wet colors cannot be integrated into his final work. Then he takes the silver dollar he has spent weeks honing to scalpel sharpness and separates the limpness of her at every natural break. The pieces are light but maneuver stiffly in his hands as he places them in rhythm: hands to feet, humerus to upper thigh, shins to forearms. Head and torso are paired by the symmetry they enjoyed in life. The torso made the body go. The head made it all go.

The symmetry is as satisfying as he imagined.

His work complete, Lo notes the descent of a fluttering hope he has not felt before. This is an assemblage Rauschenberg might have been proud of if that long dead artist had had the courage of the knife and not the blow torch. Standing in the quiet Water Builder's yard, hands and chest and belly covered in Harlem's now lusterless blood Lo wonders: Is he finally free of the directives of his selected donors? He looks up into the lowering orange of the day. The unimpressed sky is his first critic.

The air bristles. The air hums.

Harlem's owners will not mourn. They will not even eulogize her. Nobody mourns the demise of a Build. Especially one dispatched by another Build. The only thing they will worry over is the time they lost waiting for Harlem to mature into something interesting. They will file a proprietary claim with their GCT insurance liaison, pop a bottle of atomically printed '51 Chateau Margaux and discuss modifications to their next Build Child investment. They will clear her Shelf of resin trays and mirrors. When they finally agree on aesthetic attributes (opting this time for a creature of more atonal leanings), they will pay a small fortune for one of Twyla Tharp's vacuum-archived leotards and have their murdered daughter reconstituted.

The boy they will send to me.

They send Lo to me for the simple and glaring reason that I am not in a position to deny him. The thirty-three citizens of Wiloughby know I share their privilege, that I was raised and nurtured by the automated nanny prototype that would eventually raise and nurture all of them. But they think I murdered their God.

All I really did was admit to killing my own mother.

My mother did nothing short of rewriting the way the world works. She put herself on the map when she invented the ©*Pumpkin*, the first fully functional bio-interface nano computer. But she changed the world when she created the ©*Godmother* application.

What was the world like before ©*Godmother*? What was the world like before the Feed? Driving before Google Maps? Fucking before Tinder? (If you will indulge some anachronistic examples.) She brought into the world a search engine for one's life. At age ten you decided you wanted to be a day trader, or a neurosurgeon, or a ballet dancer. ©*Godmother* told you how. It held your hand, your attention, the tiny but protean seed of your intractably bright future in its welcoming graphics and careful prompts. It began with a kid-friendly anime that outlined in simple narrative with your own flattering avatar the particulars of any given profession. Games, videos, and kindly persuasive talking heads followed. As the child matured, and his or her goals became solidified, so did the app's suggestions. It took you step by step, listing educational requirements, necessary social connections, and salary projections. As you chose your path, ©*Godmother* helped clear the debris. It told you what middle school to attend in your area, what hobbies you should engage in, what summer camps to get into, what to ask for for Christmas. It helped with homework, dating, rivalries of every kind, listing and reminding relevant colleges and universities and how to meet their specific requirements. She taught you how to dress, what to eat, how to drink, both recreationally and professionally, and, upon graduation, it set up job interviews, going so far as to give you personal insights into prospective employers. It informed you of your potential employer's code of banter, their favorite jokes, how to lie about your golf handicap.

©*Godmother* made dreams come true.

And what happened when two or ten thousand people all wanted the same things? ©*Godmother* made the call. She ran the personality index projections, made the ambition and relative intelligence calculations, and in the brightness of new dawn she would whisper in your own voice what life really had in store for you.

And you accepted it. Embraced it as if it had been your most cherished desire all along. Because the world trusted my mother. Because my mother had effectively abolished greed. She made it a stipulation that her app be free of all advertising. Because in hundreds of privately per-viewed and publicly viewed demonstrations, she proved her application worked completely untethered to corporate positioning but ran solely on logic and what she termed "the natural hierarchies of existence as evidenced by the death of the illusion of free will." And her app didn't cost the public a dime. It was pretty simple, really. Monetization of her app fell squarely on the shoulders of distribution vectors. Corporations, she reasoned, would pay handsomely for human resources who had been nurtured since first cognition to a gain of functional acuity that might rival the most germ warfare-minded virologists.

I was twelve years old when ©*Godmother* finally left beta. Just a couple of months older than that when I said I murdered her.

I was already a veteran of countless fucked up nights smoking Marley Golds with my trophy dad in our VR room, and my judgment was as tweaked as my affection for him. My dad banked on the fact I was underage, so even for so ominous a capital crime, I would do little more than a few easy years in some Calabasas juvenile home. That had all been part of his plan. What he hadn't planned on was the darkness that would grow in me, the hot tar stink that would forever waft off me for having murdered the world's only branded god.

Living here in the red rock sandbox of Wiloughby, cooking for and cleaning up after people who will never possess even a quarter of my notoriety was not my choice. It was because I was welcome nowhere else on Earth. But they don't send the boy to me because we share similar crimes. Such a pairing lacks finesse. Lacks potential in pulling the "environmental trigger" as Carlos, the creator of the Build program, CEO of Wiloughby, is fond of saying. And Carlos Yakamura makes all the final choices up here.

Lo comes to me because I am a cook. Because every night of the week, adding flavor and spice, I unleash remembered dishes onto thirty-two clean and identical white china plates. And, according to Carlos Yakamura, the boy, like my atomically printed groceries, is in desperate need of seasoning.

Everybody has an angle, works a gimmick. Even cooks. Even geneticists like Carlos Yakamura. I don't just chuck a bunch of raw protein and vegetable cellulose in a pan and toss it around with a brick of butter and salt any more than Carlos withholds just insulin genes or tickles junk DNA. Up here I've come to be known by the somewhat unsavory term of "gastric archeologist." One of the first things Carlos Yakamura told me when he agreed to shuttle me up to Mars was that consciousness is not forged from sensory input alone. Reality isn't cobbled together from what we see, touch, or taste. Reality is almost entirely a product of what we *remember* seeing, touching, and tasting.

Memory is faulty. As every great con artist knows, what is faulty can be profitably manipulated. In short, what I share with Carlos Yakamura is that I am no less a forger than he. While Carlos Yakamura offers solace to his abandoned peptide bonds with superstar proteins culled from long dead innovators, I flavor my dishes with your archived memories. The sweet nostalgic pride slightly soured with motherly dread you tasted along with your Waldorf salad at your daughter's baby shower. The brothy salt of invincibility you savored with your Wagyu cowboy chop after your first hostile corporate takeover. But I can no sooner actually deliver on my claims than Carlos Yakamura could make you the proud papa of a reconstituted Nikola Tesla. That's where the artistry comes in, in what he calls "emotional veracity," the sizzle in the steak of a compromised approximation. Carlos Yakamura sends Lo to me because he knows what I can do with him: I can bring out his real and profound flavor. Builds have a complicated relationship with memories of their own, and to make the boy palatable I will have to risk braising and perhaps burning myself in the process.

Chapter 2

You can't tell the rich what to do. That's why the rich feel rich. And they won't dump an investment unless it has both proven fiscally and socially unprofitable. Lo is a major investment but one that exists, like all the Builds on Wiloughby, as a social lure. A creature whose talent and performance give the owner bragging rights and some social standing. That's why the boy's owners don't come to me right away to pawn him off. They have to be sure the boy's stock has actually fallen past recoupment. They first visit the owners of the murdered girl, an asset evaluation, an adjustment of liability, cunningly disguised as a casual cocktail gathering.

Wiloughby is based on a version of home. What the chronically rich call home. The bloated clapboards of East Hampton. The sugar-cubed villas of Lake Como, the flat mid-century roofs of the Hollywood Hills. These houses (and the hedonistic lifestyle they engender) are the real reasons those who can afford it come to Wiloughby. You simply could not build such vacuous monstrosities back on Earth, not in the coastal Eco-Liberal confederacies from where they all came. They are old money.

Once in a while, the architecture here might surprise you.

There's a beautiful six bedroom, five and a half baths, for instance, built in the sensuous, gyno-floral style of Zaha Hadid a gay couple once shared with their now-butchered Build daughter. The home revels in the awe generated by all things that are based on small things but have been blown totally out of proportion. In this case, the house resembles nothing less than an enormous white orchid in delicate and static bloom. The owners know property. They made their fortune in real estate. Their last deal of note was brokering the sale of NASA to the entertainment conglomerate that still has the ironic audacity to use a cartoon rodent as its logo. It is to this house Lo's owners have come, armed with not only a twenty-thousand credit bottle of vintage Japanese whiskey, but with the boy himself. They know the girl was covered and they can only guess what her demise will do to their hosts' GCT insurance premium. So they've come knowing the real olive branch is a painting of their daughter, the one they have insisted Lo paint.

They've insisted on oil, not the quick watercolors he does for their other guests, a party trick.

It's the least they can do.

They haven't bothered to look at it. Just like they didn't bother to follow Lo to the Water Builder's yard to behold his artistic progress the evening Harlem was killed. Lo's owners have even postponed their game, have come in their own skins (which they are sure will let their hosts know just how seriously they take their boy's recent behavior).

They look youthful and slim and slightly predatory, plain by their standards. On his toned frame, the husband wears a celluloid collar and tight tweed suit he's printed from a nineteenth- century Lock and Co. catalogue. His wife wears a vintage Balenciaga minidress airily re-imagined in puce ostrich down that shows her shapely thighs and calves. His collar chafes. Her feathers tickle. Lo, somber and removed, wears his Build-blue overalls just like he does every day. They take a deep breath of manufactured air before they ring the doorbell. Just enough to calm their nerves and berate the boy one last time before they enter.

I'm proud of that air.

I've scented it myself.

Mars is a frozen and rusty planet whose native odor, if the probes can be trusted, is something like the smell of a cold, but well-seasoned cast iron pan. Scrubbed air is breathable, but hardly inspiring, and so I worked hard to get the smell right. I took my cue from the long and empty russet landscapes, the blood-ochre cliffs and yellow ochre gullies that would make anyone think of the Western deserts back home, of sage and blooming piñon and the cozy-smelling smoke of burning mesquite. But the rich don't like deserts now that most of Earth is one. They prefer a view they can associate with opportunity and abundant liquidity, a view of water even if they are forbidden to drink or bathe in it back on Earth.

So I was forced to change it.

It's sea air you smell now—a high, clear, ion-rich ether of living salt, cut with just a hint of hot tar and wind-worn wood.

People love it.

But I don't like its inauthentic quality; the lie that goads your lungs (and spirit) to the peace and solitude of a beach that never arrives.

They ring the bell. The door opens and the boy watches as they enter. He is disappointed. The house is really nothing more than a shell that garages a series of movable psychotomimetic tryptamine screens.

Today these screens have decided we are in a villa on Venice's Grand Canal. If not comfortable, at least Lo is familiar with the room. He remembers his genetic actuating files from when Singer-Sargent had choked on his absinthe while drinking with his rival Giovanni Boldini on this villa's balcony. (That social faux-pas had cost Sargent his bid to paint the bizarre Italian socialite Luisa Casati and sent him, penniless and dejected, back to Fifth Avenue.) The room has not changed. The walls are the color of dead white cake, all baroque worry and bland frescoes. There is a "window" that opens onto the "canal" from which Lo can see the rancid sea chopping grayly against the failing foundations of similarly exhausted and slumping villas. He can even smell the stink of rotting fish from rotating misters in the corners of the room. The stifling Mediterranean air can barely lift the disembodied cries of gondoliers to his ears. Lo is impressed by the immersive quality of the shared hallucination he is experiencing. Harlem's folks spared no expense in the tryptamine synthesis of their screen's pixels. Even the furniture looks substantial, desiccated velvets and carved wood with flaking gold.

But he is not asked to sit.

These people hold no aesthetic interest for Lo.

Lo watches, holding his canvas, while one of Harlem's dads steps forward to kiss the air that hovers near the cheeks and hairlines of his owners. He is seal-slick in a black jumpsuit that rainbows like fresh oil as it clings to his sculpted chest and thighs. Harlem's other father is dressed identically as he offers only his hand to his guests. Lo thinks they look ridiculous but functional like English Channel swimmers or Japanese puppeteers and he is slightly embarrassed by the flamboyance of his owners' clothes. The whiskey is accepted, briefly admired but stays unopened when it is placed like any other bric-a-brac on the villa's ornate occasional table. Faces smile and nod but their eyes stay poker sharp. The first thing one of Lo's owners says after they sit, and she says this in a cloying babyish voice, as if her request couldn't possibly be an imposition, as if her hosts wouldn't mind changing the scene.

"The fish smell is making me positively ill. Would you mind terribly?"

The murdered girl's dads comply immediately.

In a flash, the air freshens as the canal out the window becomes the one in Amsterdam during a Cold War mid-autumn. The furniture and walls follow suit, shedding their threadbare velvet for sleek Swedish teak and folksy macramé wall hangings in gamey smelling Norwegian wool. A demure fire sparks to life in its Swedish modern grate. Lo's male owner crosses to the unopened whiskey, cracking the seal, while he asks his hosts where they hide their glasses.

"This shit's about as old as it's going to get," he says, holding the open bottle. "Might as well crank it back now that it's not so stifling in here."

Harlem's dads smile coldly as one of them places four slanted Eva Solo whiskey glasses on the smooth teak of the Kofod-Larsen coffee table that flickers then solidifies slowly from the low-piled carpeting that separates the two couples.

Getting the girl's owners to comply has put them strategically on the defensive, all the proof Lo's owners need that their social standing is still intact. The girl's murder is assumed to be a teenaged misunderstanding. An unfortunate delay in familial cohesiveness.

"I suppose Harlem always was a little naive in matters of the heart," one of her fathers says.

"Oh, I agree," Lo's female owner offers. "A romantic disposition can be such a liability. Especially in a modern girl."

"Let's hope we have better luck with the next one," Harlem's other dad says pouring two fingers worth of whiskey into each of the tumblers.

The rest will be easy for Lo's owners.

Sips of whiskey and muttered apologies about the inconvenience they had caused, enlivened by questions about the particulars of the new Build that will replace their dead daughter. The conversation lightens, becomes chatty.

Lo's owners become so confident that they and Lo are forgiven that they risk a snarky turn when they hear about their hosts' plans for the modified personality for their new Build.

"Twyla Tharp? Really? A little too weedy for my tastes. Why not Mark Morris or at least Merce Cunningham? But then you risk the foibles of an actual innovator. Truly gifted men can be so *bitchy*."

Social dominance is never telegraphed, not when it counts.

That Lo's owners know they have gotten what they came for is lost on the boy. He only knows he's hearing his name called. Snapping fingers, a few disparaging remarks directed at him, softened with light chuckles, and Lo is turning his canvas around to face the crowd.

The room is silent, but the mood is in full free fall.

He doesn't understand. He's proud of his painting. The looser technique, the Fauvist colors. It represents yet another turn in direction for him.

When Lo bothers to look up into their eyes they are shards of icy contempt.

"I thought you said your kid was selected from the *masters*," one of the murdered girl's fathers sneers. "Not some masochistic mid-century *hack* like *Francis fucking Bacon*!"

How has Lo offended? He wasn't going for Bacon. Just something that would offset the dreary dun color of their walls. Lo is confused. But Lo is often confused. He looks at his work. Yes. That's her. Perfection. Just like he left her in the Water Builder's yard.

He has painted her in stacked glassine chunks, more fully herself than whenever she moved. Her face in earthy greens and in tender repose. He'd been going for a little pre-Renaissance saintly martyrdom here. Now Harlem's fathers are screaming. Lo feels a slight tingle a shame. He should be lowering his head and apologizing like his genes have been selected for him to do. But he doesn't. Something in him cools his shame, blanches the blush in his cheeks to the neutral color of the walls.

The canvas is ripped from his hands, smashed against the avocado hood of their Malm fireplace. Lo is yanked by his arm, one owner seething, another smeared with tears and choking mucus.

"How could you let him humiliate us like this?" one father rants.

"I thought we were getting a memorial portrait not some snap of a view through a *deli* case," the other moans, the moisture flowing from his enraged head beading on the fabric of his ridiculous jumpsuit.

"How could you let him create that *horror*?"

And what is the boy thinking deep in the damp layers of his mind? Fury? Pride? Remorse? No. Nothing. The boy thinks nothing. His work has spoken for itself.

Chapter 3

My first meeting with the boy's owners is terse. It's a curt release of liability that is negotiated one afternoon at an empty four-top in my cafe, The Church. They come unannounced, catch me tit-deep in the evening's preparations. I've got most of the dinners ready for printing but I still need to tweak Mr. and Mrs. Shorenstein's bouillabaisse—sourced from a room service meal they had on their honeymoon in the south of France. I'm pretty sure I've nailed the balance of sweet-anticipated pleasure and the acidity of wedding night performance anxiety but the salinity of late twentieth-century *Juan-les-Pins* snapper is proving problematic.

From the kitchen, I see them come in, a hard looking fifty-something blonde whose gullied face and deflated (but still flourishing) breasts tell me she's spent the best years of her life working for tips on the pole. Her husband looks like some par-baked nickel-and-dime boxer, all busted nose and knuckles floating in reams of flabby bulk.

I scurry out, still in my apron, plate in hand, and try to appear interested. I offer them my newly hatched blue tomatoes, goat milk burrata I make from Lily's milk with a drizzle of friction-brewed balsamic.

They refuse. They haven't come to snack.

They simply want to be rid of the boy.

They can't risk his paint brush on their dinner guests now.

"Just take him," they say. "He could be of use to you around here." They're pretty sure they can recoup the majority of their initial investment in him. A Behavior Modification Anomaly claim is worth the rise in their insurance premium. The rest they can make up in child credits when they claim him as a "natural dependent" on their next quarter taxes.

"He could sketch the diners between courses. Singer-Sargent watercolors. Or Renaissance tempera, if you can spare the eggs," they say.

"He'll do anything," one of them croaks. "Muck out the meat printer. Haul the compost."

"Julienne the guests?" I smirk.

They harden. They are losing their patience. And I know why. I can smell it on their skin. They want desperately to get back to their game.

My first night in detention outside of Los Angeles, I was allowed dinner with the warden and his wife. Even among the inmates pre-teen bitcoin hackers and ransomware gangsters I was pretty hot shit. I was seated next to the warden's wife, a plump and plain looking woman who made no attempt to soften the tracks of all forty of her years. It was only when I felt the damp lump of her hand on my knee during our wedge salads that I figured out the seating arrangements had been her choice.

What followed was a sad parade of chores and odd jobs: busboy at their VIP lunches, small personal errands that got me out of group meditation—anything to get me near her. Her awkward insistence and my boyish deferrals became a kind of idiotic tango with us.

Then one night, I was surprised to find myself alone in the detention center's Himalayan salt sauna. Briny heat and amber glow, and then a small rush of coolness as the door to the sauna was opened. I looked up as it closed. Backlit there in front of the dry cedar door was the most gorgeous girl I could have imagined.

And that should have been clue enough as to what was happening.

For she was not *like* a girl I had imaged. She was *exactly* as I had imagined her. A pin-up Pacific Islander in touristy grass skirt and nothing else. Small, dark complected with black sparkling eyes and an erotic yet innocent grace in her hips. Breasts too small and capable for most twelve-year-old fantasies. The girl I'd seen sashay topless on the desert-island shore countless afternoons on the massive reality enhancement screens in my dad's separate bedroom. When we had nothing to say or do with one another, we would get high together and watch her dance.

But the smell of the girl in the sauna, enlivened in the heat, was not the salty gardenia scent mixed with pot smoke I'd shared with my dad.

Burnt bubblegum and boiled cabbage. A clutch of disgust jammed into my lust.

The cooling skin of a full body graft job.

It was the warden's wife enshrined in her last desperate gambit: I was to make her feel wanted again while the warden's wife would wear my island cutie's skin.

It's the same with Lo's owners. The same sad stab of despair I remember as I tipped the warden's wife on her back. I swallow hard and ask about the boy's unusual name.

"Lo?"

They show me on my ©*Pumpkin:*

My retinal vaults bleed with the dull view of another room. It doesn't smell like revolution in there. Stale coffee and institutional outgassing. Unpampered hair and the hot circuit funk of military grade CPUs. The Bruin calendar on the wall reads October 1969. In an instant, the provenance of the boy's name emerges from the flurry of advancing and retreating sensations inside my skull.

We're at UCLA, less than two hours to midnight on the twenty-ninth. The first message ever sent across the silk of what will one day be the real (and very worn) web, what we now call the Feed. Stanford had tried to send the world's first internet message, but the cursor had stopped after the "L" and the "O," failing to transmit the "G."

"Good thing Stanford never got the 'G'," I say wryly, "or your kid might have just been lazy."

Carlos Yakamura has given me nothing about the boy when he "suggested" I take him after Harlem's death.

I want a little history from the boy's owners, a vague understanding at least of what I'm getting myself into before I agree to take him. They shift in their seats and try not to audibly sigh. Like I said, they are anxious to get back to their game.

Just that morning she had suggested a body change.

"Let's be Babe and Bunny," she had said over their printed buckwheat bagels and smear. She'd found some great vintage files from 1947, post-war black and whites of this "insane" looking couple in front of a Venice, California bar. He will be Babe, a retired middleweight with a face like desiccated bread dough and hands so swollen he can no longer make a fist and she will be Bunny. A once dazzling blonde with a funky uterine bulge that says she's comfortable with what allure she has left. We can print some Lucky Strikes. Or Chesterfield Kings and hump in a cramped little room over the saloon floor. She's done all the research. Half the bar has already been extruded in their living room.

"Tell me about the boy," I ask.

He picks at a dollop of cheese with his newly minted dock worker fingers and she cracks the crow's feet at the corners of her eyes, cautiously, like breaking in a new pair of real leather Louboutin pumps and shows me her cosmetically yellowed teeth.

"This should never have happened," Bunny says, staining her tanned fingers in the fresh ink of her pack of Lucky Strikes.

"We were careful," Babe croaks. "We spent months reading biographies, scanning monographs of famous artists. We settled on Sargent and Masaccio. We didn't want anything too maudlin. Guess Yakamura missed the mark."

"Where did you get the gametes?" I ask, having heard Carlos Yakamura use the term in his explanation of the Build process.

"We got a viable scraping from one of Sargent's walking sticks when it came up at the Viscaya estate auction in Miami," he says, his surprise at my question coming off more accusatory than clarifying in his now-crude persona. "Masaccio was harder. We finally bribed one of the nuns who curates at the Casica di Reggello. She'd heard a rumor that Masaccio had nicked himself with a trowel while doing the *Triptych* there."

"We cut that with alpha intelligence and standard insecurity coding." Stands to reason. You'd want your investment docile and always eager to please. "Pretty basic boutique mix." She slurps a gobbet of my famous cheese. "Hey, that shit's not bad," she says. "How'd you wrangle an actual *goat* up here?" She grins. I stay frosty.

"So what do you think went wrong?" I ask, only slightly amused.

She lips the butt of her smoke. To light a match would be keeping with their ruse but would doom us all in this shakily built air we're breathing. Without a flame, the tip of her cigarette oranges in increments as she inhales. I smirk again. The smoke smells like steamed cauliflower. She exhales and looks longingly at the muscle gone to flab on her husband's gut.

"Yakamura says the kid's just maturing into his angry postmodernist phase. Nothing went wrong," he says. "We paid for a realist." He's sloppy with his consonants. South Boston. Maybe post-war Brooklyn and I wonder if the vintage Brando was part of the seed file or his own irresistible affectation.

"He's an amazing kid, though," she adds, forming the words carefully through the virgin geography of her jaw. "Just lives to please."

My custody of the kid is already a done deal, but I've come to hate all these elitist, body swapping bastards on Wiloughby, and I want to make them earn it.

"You two just don't care for his latest aesthetic direction. Is that it?" I ask. I hope they're wishing they had waited to strap on these meat suits of theirs. For their neglected bodies with their dappling of age spots are doing little to augment the persuasiveness of their case. She reassesses her argument and toys with a bruise-colored slab of tomato before she switches her tack to one of persuasive nostalgia.

"We'd have these dinner parties. Al fresco, you know?" she begins, clearing her smoker's throat. "In the spring when they launch the atmosphere scrubbers and the evening sky turns that kind of opal color? Lo would come out after the aperitifs and sketch the guests. Do some quick watercolors. They'd dry in the hot breezes of the sulfur buffers. Our friends loved them." Their nostalgia pretty much sickens me.

"And what did you do with him when he wasn't acting like a trained seal?"

"Sorry?"

Their faces go a tandem blank. My reference is too obscure. I keep forgetting how old I am.

"What did you do with him when he was done entertaining your guests?"

"Same thing you do with the rest of them, I guess," he mumbles. "Hit the beta remote and put him on the Shelf."

I can imagine the boy there in the murk. The four small walls of his closet they call a "Shelf" flecked with watery red and yellow and green, all gray now in the dark. How much room did they afford him? Just enough to hide him? Enough to keep those expensive pulmonary organs fit and ready for service? I haven't even met the kid but I'm beginning to feel for him.

You're not going to leave me here, Dad.

Just overnight, Cookie. Just until we get this thing figured out.

But dad…

I feel bad for the Builds. Having never crowned from the folds of a mother, these boutique kids never compromised their owner's hearts with real affection. They were conceived in glass, toasted with plastic but always drank from paper.

Wasn't that the real reason Carlos Yakamura had flocked to Mars, to a place called Wiloughby, where the Declaration of Helsinki (that banned such genetic experiments) thins to nothing once past the Earth's troposphere?

I smile. Offer a parting drink.

"Boilermaker? Scotch neat?" Something keeping with the theme of their latest masquerade. But they refuse. They've said all they came to say. And I haven't really been asked.

SECONDARY MODERN

Chapter 4

To understand why Wiloughby exists, you must first remember what happened on first-world Earth. Drexler's dream of unlimited abundance was ultimately realized but with strings. What was supposed to be Earth's nanotech revolution was a fart in a bathtub of crippling international regulation and proprietary intelligence. When it became possible for home atomic printers to spit out everything from deli-worthy corned beef to vintage Balenciaga gowns, every national and local legislature called foul in various regional accents.

The black market toiled under the generalist's dilemma, not knowing what to print more of: soy-polymer handguns or guava-flavored methamphetamine.

Strategic preservationists whimpered about money motivating mundane actions while ecological fascists stole an industrial atomic printer and flooded Monsanto's Midwestern seed modifying laboratory with twelve million gallons of ripe and beautifully rendered pig piss.

There were fail-safes, of course, ever weakening firewalls that prevented jihadists and more homegrown haters from printing weapons-grade plutonium on their aftermarket actuators in the wicked light of their West Bank mud huts or South Carolina weatherboard shacks. But it was just a matter of time before the genie of radical ideology would thread his way through the twisted flute of his bottle and grant us all total destruction.

We looked where we always look when common sense and social tolerance fail us: to tech.

Tech would save us. Cold, clean, magically rational tech would unify us. But *whose* tech?

There were two schools of thought back then on fatally fucked up Earth, both as radical in their ways as the cultural prejudices they were so generously and privately funded to prevent. One school (the old school some might say) was hard tech. This was my mother's alma mater. Better machines had clearly just led to better threats, she reasoned. So, it wasn't a savior of automated baristas and car assembly robots she favored.

Access to what made the machines *go* was her answer.

She knew her history, could quote her Orwell and knew that to succeed, she had to take humanity out of the equation. *A single unified operating system based on unbiased multi-phasic mathematical algorithms* that breathed when we breathed and slept when we slept and guided us with a cool but supremely rational hand through our lives.

©*Godmother.*

That was her hope.

Her rival on the field was Carlos Yakamura, who didn't believe in computers. Not as the causal factors in human destiny, anyway. He had put his faith in people.

Computers, he reasoned, had been the beneficiaries of relentless hourly evolution for hundreds of years while we had hardly improved since the day we shuffled out of the caves of Lascaux and started raping Neanderthals. Why build a better tool, he muttered sullenly from the clutter of his gene sequencers and protein-peptide actuators, when we had finally come to the place where we could actually make a more empathetic, intelligent, and ultimately more loving carpenter?

And when all that shit went down with GERI, the Ukrainian AI service drone, when the machine's leaked cognitive files had proved that machines could be as abused and subjugated as people, it looked, for a moment, like he might have his way. But hard tech proved as resilient and ultimately squeamish as us. The world saw what happened to poor GERI as a call to eliminate every temptation to create another slave class. And gene tech, for all its glowing trans-humanist claims, was seen as the surest path that would lead some, if not all of us, back to the antebellum plantation and the field overseer.

Carlos Yakamura lost his funding when behavioral genetic manipulation was banned. My mother became a multi-billionaire. For a time, the world seemed safe.

The first thing ©*Godmother* did was recognize the potential harm in several illogical substances. Access to everything from hydrogenated cooking oils to smart bombs was categorically denied. But the passionless equalitarian math my mother had based her system on was still indifferent to illogical impulses like racial or social injustice.

She found out early it was very difficult to calibrate a unified system on a constantly fluctuating baseline. Standpoint epistemology and evidence-based truth were in a constant food fight of mushy memes and sticky collapsed nuance. Everyone was getting dirty. Then she realized her attempts at unity were the problem. Unity is hard, unbending. Only division allowed for real freedom and fluidity. A house divided was precisely why it stood. Only a system of conflicting ideas dependent upon their mutually intrenched positions would give stability. That's when she had her breakthrough. Only when her system took *regional* memes for its baseline was it a hit. What was "normal" in Los Angeles or Tel Aviv was unthinkable in Charlottesville or the Sudan.

So, while the world was saved from mutual destruction, it could still hate.

People were still people after all, despite the bitter roots of their particular confirmation biases.

Nations dissolved into factions of shared consensus. America opened up along ancient (if predictable) ideological fault lines and limped into its Second Secession, and Carlos Yakamura and thirty-two other of his super-solvent and fed-up followers muscled past their last gulps of de-salinated water and leased a commercial planetary shuttle and craned their monied necks to a red dot just east of Venus.

Chapter 5

I didn't know what the fuck Carlos Yakamura was supposed to be the first time I saw him.

Up to that point, all our communications, culminating in his "invitation" that I could open a restaurant on Wiloughby, had been text-based only.

So, when I saw him slink on four articulated paws into an empty two top at The Church, I was truly stymied. This is Wiloughby's CEO? What the hell is he supposed to be? Some rich kid's bio-bot gone rogue?

But there were no children in the streets of Wiloughby then.

I didn't know that I was a hero of sorts to him, that I had effectively declared him victor on the clay courts of high tech by effectively removing his rival when I killed my own mother.

I hadn't bothered to ©*Godmother* his wealth before my arrival. Let's just say he did all right. Earth might have prohibited what his gene therapy could do to the souls of its tax-paying citizens, but it had no problem allowing him to alter what was on their surface.

Centromere Reclamation Therapy he called it.

If you've ever looked into the eyes of a seemingly virile man or super-sexy woman but were conflicted at the subtle sadness and resignation you saw in those eyes before they said yes to a dirty martini or screamed before an orgasm, you have Carlos Yakamura to thank for your confusion.

No one who could afford it looked their ages anymore.

Birthdays became as uncelebrated as Arbor Days on a desert planet.

I was ignorant of his bout with ALS that had finally forced all his synaptic fanfare into a two-note drone of binomial code that could fit into a processor the size of a single grain of smelt roe.

I had never heard of "ambient consciousness," much less flirted with the option. To have oneself effectively canned in the aluminum carbide skull of a mechanical nine tailed fox wasn't in vogue.

A *kitsune,* Carlos Yakamura had called the metal animal shell that housed his mind.

During our first meeting, I had poured him a passable Montrachet and went to go "fire" the *uni*-infused pork shoulder he'd once bought off a Santa Monica food truck the night of his first French kiss. When I served him, I was amazed to see him balance on the lobster-like plumage of his fanning tails and pick up the knife and fork in his tiny claws and actually feed himself. Maybe amazed is too strong a word. I was engaged. Amused.

The kind of cheap delight you get the first time you see one of those crappy CRISPR/Cas 9 pterodactyls circle the sunglass kiosk before shitting multicolored PEZ all over the mall floor.

Then he started talking, and my amusement ripened to something darker. His voice was a pleasant shock, warm, resonate, and seductive—not at all diminished by the tiny servos and metallic rinds that passed for his lips.

"There he is," he had greeted me on our first encounter. "My knight in shining toque!" I didn't wear a toque.

"Chef's hats," I answered sullenly, "are worn only in real kitchens not in labs." He grinned, showing me the small tines of his chromed teeth.

"Now, Cook. It is only within prescribed limits that real innovation can ripen."

He talked shop in a language he thought I could understand. He likened losing weight by shunting the insulin-fat gene to reducing rosemary essence in balsamic to mellow its bitterness. He called intelligence "a neural connective cassoulet," clarifying archly that opting for cognitive capability oddly selected against higher limbic functions. In other words: First we become smart, then empathetic. Selection without environmental pressures is in fact selection *in spite of* environmental factors and runs the risk of zero adaptability.

But I understood, didn't I?

Every beer drinker forgives the crimes of yeast, doesn't he? No one reprimands what is resurrected from a coffin of Carrera marble with a lid of pork fat if that once vibrant haunch can now be called Parma ham.

Weren't all culinary classics just savory embalming?

His meal ended, Carlos Yakamura killed he last sip of his wine and leaned back contentedly against the shiny plumage of all nine of his tails.

"The application of science is ultimately irrelevant," he began in a far-away tone. "Good, bad, or indifferent, what the world does with what we discover is up to the highest bidder. Why? Because science itself is really a kind of larceny. We steal secrets, Cook," he said, looking up at me with his tiny black eyes. "We rummage around in God's sock drawer, if you will, mining for the dirty little impulses that make us. And for that to thrive, for science to thrive, society must engender a level of moral ambiguity. I'm not saying anything new here. This is how all scientists feel when the microphones are off, and funding is in place. We just want to *know*. The way any artist just wants to know. We just want to try stuff. We don't care why. We can't. Not if we want to do something miraculous."

I didn't know it then. (How could I?) But all of Carlos' *laissez faire* bullshit was just that. The metal fox had a plan. A very real plan for the boy he would one day hand over to me. He had been prepping me for the difficulty of the boy's late surrogacy even before I knew I'd one day grow to love him.

HARLEM NOCTURNE

Chapter 6

Harlem Kant, the girl Lo had murdered, was what comes when hysterical visions of dexterity ferment in the cramped dimensions of a plain, relentlessly freckled girl. She had been selected with a slight excess in the length of her thighs, which gave her an almost awkward, flightless look when not in motion. But once the music started, she was completely transformed. To say her dancing was hypnotic was not a metaphor. She was a literal mesmerist. A feminine hallucinogenic that used movement as a delivery system instead of blotter paper or shrooms.

She moved impossibly slow, in achingly suspended adagios that made you think you were watching her underwater. Even her hair seemed to sway away from her head like tendrils of lake-swallowed reeds. You felt an encroaching but yearned for peace when you watched her. Like the darkening euphoria described by drowning victims before they succumb to the depths.

Her prime motivators had been culled from samples taken from the wool of one of Pavlova's autographed pointe shoes, but the rest was a clever combination of opposites. An innate musicality balanced with just enough teenaged self-loathing to keep her disciplined.

I had met Harlem only a few times, only during the rehearsals for the biannual launching of the atmosphere scrubbers, when the citizens of Wiloughby would gather for what passed as a showcase. I used to bring the performers snacks of cubed water and nori sticks, and I watched them as they calmly churned through the skills that justified keeping them fed. Their meal tickets.

My God, the young Builds were peaceful creatures. Their serene faces never betraying the incredible burden of focus they must have been shifting. Peaceful but spooky. Peaceful in the practice of their talents, but spooky in their expression. The way Harlem could soothe you to the core just with her gestures, the others, too, had abilities that seemed classic enough but more than bordered on particle physics.

While there had been dozens at first, there were now just four Builds including Lo.

There was Isaac ben Marcus, black as I am but darker complected with his bristling hair and barely sprouted goatee, quietly seeding his elaborate dollhouses. He had originally been selected from the British sculptor Henry Moore. His bio-directives had been so faithful that his owners had been able to profit quite nicely by dealing in off-world forgeries. When Isaac learned of this, he just shifted focus to construction techniques. In fact, it was his innovations with carbon peptides that had allowed for the construction of my farmhouse.

He was only fifteen.

Trilla McNeil at just ten, was the youngest of the Builds. Cacophonously seeded from samples of Liszt and John Cage, she had been selected for a four-octave splay that left her with hands like leaf rakes. She was caramel skinned like me, with Polynesian features and kinky black hair that flared around her sensuous face when she played her keyboard.

But it wasn't just music she played. Some music can move you but none that I know of can actually change the weather.

I remember at one launching of the air scrubbers during the winter solstice when all but me were in such denial as to the season, she had actually made it snow with her atonal rendition of "Jingle Bells."

The only time I remember seeing Lo was at rehearsals for their summer recital. Trilla and Harlem had been at it for weeks, Trilla having composed a special variation on the *Allure Cola* jingle that Harlem had agreed to enliven with movement. Trilla's music had made it rain.

It was to be Harlem's last dance.

I had only looked at Lo because he was looking so loudly at Harlem. I don't know how else to describe it. The look on the boy's face as Harlem moved in front of him had been as loud as an air horn at a stadium game. And just as difficult to ignore. Harlem had kept slipping in Trilla's puddles and Trilla was trying to regulate the rhythm of her rainfall, but Lo's eyes never left the belly-white blur of the dancer. He didn't even bother to look down at his sketch. His owners were at the rehearsal. Owners often were. But they were always chatting among themselves, like classic stage mothers, when they came. Harlem's owners must have assumed he was struggling to develop his own artistic voice. Why else was he tearing page after scribbled page out of his sketchbook? They didn't realize his fixation on her had emboldened his eyes to such an extent that his new frontier, his new first principal, was rapidly developing into a sculptural repurposing of their daughter. If they had heard the look on his face, there would have been no doubt as to his intentions.

THE CHURCH OF BUZZ ALDRIN

Chapter 7

Lo comes to me on Christmas Day at the pinking of the solar perigee. We once called it sunset. He comes unescorted—undelivered—alone as if he was just out for a stroll and had stopped by to say hello.

Hello to a perfect stranger.

No one cares that it's Christmas. The people of Wiloughby insisted on an inclusive secularly social atmosphere, and so they junked the holiday with the same entitled whimsy of the emperor who excepted the pagan ritual in the first place.

But I remember Christmas before half the country seceded from the Union, when you could still garnish and anticipate the day in America without people thinking your white meat and nog were spiked with Christian privilege and socio-religious insensitivity.

There are no trees on Wiloughby. And I couldn't convince myself to print a plastic spruce just so I could hang stuff on it. I have a bulby stalk drooping in the corner whose sprouts pulse red and green with bio-luminescent algae. Empty protein tubes are strung over the door frames as a sadly festive garland. I'm baking gingerbread men.

I am alerted to Lo at my gate by the warning clucks of my chickens. He's come to the back door. I look out my kitchen window, and there past the pickets is the tall question-marked shape of the boy. His dark eyes scan the misters of my hanging garden, then feel the newness of my gaze and look up at me.

I don't notice his dusky good looks, his terrible posture. I only see wilderness.

That is my first impression of him. A trackless face. A face where anything could happen. I am struck at how much he resembles the lead from one of my old Hitchcock files, his knees locked at the junctures of his long legs, his dark hair cropped close on his young head. And I remember thinking, as I removed the gingerbread men from the sonic enclave, if my pampered neighbors had been acquainted with just a bit more cinematic history, they would have been wary of his proximity to showers and sharpened objects.

My cookies are warm, not hot to the touch, baked as they were with friction induction, a noisy but far too localized heat that doesn't stir into the air the scent of butter and cloves as much as I hoped. I want Lo's arrival to be special but not over orchestrated and I fear if he's ©*Godmother*ed Christmas he'll only be acquainted with mall riots, burning tinsel, and stomping deaths at old Rockefeller Center. I grab a cookie as casually as I can and head out to greet him.

"Lo?" I ask, as if he could be anyone else. "Merry Christmas."

I hand him the cookie.

He looks down at it in his open palm, his long fingers careful not to curl and obstruct his searching gaze.

"Yeah," he says with a grin. "Why are you handing me this anthropomorphic pastry?"

He says it quietly, plainly, without irony or inflection. Before I can answer he breaks into a dismissive laugh and holds the cookie up to his nose. "What do you have in there? Chinese ginger. Tunisian cinnamon." He sniffs again, a hunter sussing the spoor of unsuspecting prey. "Romanian nutmeg. And *goat* butter? That's new." I can't help but be impressed.

"Jesus. You can smell all that? Grab an apron, man."

"Merry Christmas," he mumbles, passing through the gate. "What should I call you?" he asks as he passes me. I don't like my name after a childhood of hearing it so much in the Feed so I tell him to call me what everyone calls me.

"Cook," I say to his back. "Call me Cook."

I follow him up the walk past the front door, painfully aware my welcoming overtures must seem as suspect to him as the engineered flaking of the clapboard that covers my farmhouse. I notice he has set his cookie among the ribbon book marks and old 45s that clutter my entrance table.

One leg of the gingerbread man is missing.

If he has enjoyed it, he gives no indication.

I watch his head from the back as he moves through my house, see it swivel as he takes in my pre-aged floors and rugs. He smiles at my simple couches, the divots driven into the cushions from my loafing weight, a book, butterflied, by a "snuffed" LED candle on a side table. A funky poverty museum. Just what the kid needs: another eccentric handler with a yen for conspicuous history.

He pauses at the threshold of the kitchen. I can hear him take a deep breath. I am proud of my kitchen. Like the house, it was not extruded like the others on Wiloughby. One of the perks upon which I insisted when I agreed to Carlos Yakamura's offer was a custom dwelling built from my own meticulous files.

Every sliver of grain in my wide plank floors, every fissure in the cracked pickling of my beadboard, every useless nail head and dummy peg from the front pickets to the dark splay of the water damage in my pitched attic was lovingly reassembled from three dimensional scans I'd given to Isaac ben Marcus the Build, who by that point had changed his focus from sculpture to architecture.

I don't tell him what it's really based on. No full disclosure. We're not pals yet. It's just a meme-print of an American farmhouse from the semi-prosperous American plains of the 1890s.

I watch him take in my array of hanging iron pans and dried herbs. I refuse to cook in copper. Nothing seasons like cast iron, and I know he can smell the years of melted grease and deglazing that seep from their blackened surfaces.

It's loud in here.

So loud with braided garlic and boxed onions, with strung fennel and sorrel and wild thyme and dozens of other herbs, even I can still smell it. His fingers graze the expertly rusted flange of my sink's hand-cranked water pump. He looks back to me, his eyes asking if it is safe to touch. I point to a cake of soap. He picks it up.

"You know what that is?" I ask

"Why do you still wash with water? Sonic friction is more efficient."

The old hygienic austerity of Earth came back to me like a bad taste. It's not a soothing experience, "washing" with hyper frequencies. Nothing about it would goad you into singing a cheerful song. The way the deaf probably wince at the silent hostility of a shout, a "shower," back on Earth, though silent, reprimands one clean. With sonic friction the fillings in your teeth seem to rattle and you feel slightly shamed. And when it's over, after fifteen seconds or so of mechanized scolding, you are covered in sour white flurries of your own ash that you must dry brush off to be "clean."

"Your owners didn't let you wash with water?"

"Why would they?" the boy asks, genuinely perplexed. I am saddened then dimly excited by the prospect of all the small simple pleasures I might introduce him to.

"Sonic friction doesn't smell like this." And I hold the softened block of soap to his nose.

"Is that lemon?" he asks, speaking into the bar.

"That's verbena. With a little dried rosemary." He closes his eyes, the orbs twitching under the thin lids as he tracks the care that put the scent there.

"It foams, right?" he asks, smiling finally. I smile back. He works the handle and the pump coughs up a clear cold flow. He folds the soap cake slowly between his palms, his knuckles rippling over the slowed edges. I wonder what hygiene file he's ©*Godmother*-ing. He works up a lather and places the cake back on its grate. I pump water over his hands as he rinses.

"It's doesn't burn like I thought it would." He stops suddenly, his face slightly flushed as if such unprofitable pleasure is not due him. I force a smile through my heart-break. He holds his hands, dripping, bowed at the wrists. I toss him a flour sack towel, another of my obsessive details. He dries his hands and folds the towel, draping it carefully on the lip of the sink. Then he raises his fingers to his face.

"Ashes there," he says. "And something not as sweet."

"Synth animal fat and ashes are a binding agent. You can *smell* that?"

"It smells like you actually used combustion," he nods.

"Only in my dreams."

"Well. Very convincing. Must be very difficult when one can't utilize first principals."

I flash on the bloody blocks of Harlem that I'd seen on the general solicitation Feed that gives all of us here on Wiloughby what passes for news.

And even then, standing there looking at him in the fading light of my kitchen, I could not understand why he thought that girl, Harlem, that lovely, lovely girl could better serve anyone's aesthetic principals if in pieces.

Lo straps on a faded apron.

"What do I do?" he asks, looking among the cookware.

I'm a bit nervous to give him a knife, repulsed by my reticence.

But what can I do? He's here to learn.

I pick up a thick bladed Santoku I use on non-printed produce.

"You ever chop onions?" He doesn't answer. I move to the atomic printer and feed it the specs of a common wooden kitchen match. A warning emoji in comic cross-eyed panic flashes on the read out, telling me combustible material is restricted. I okay the recommended modification with my employee number, and the machine hums dutifully and out drops a four-edged wooden sliver. The head even smells like sulphur, but I know it will never light. "You hold this between your teeth, you won't cry when you chop. You know that trick?" He fingers the wisp of pine that has never known sunlight or rain and places it between his lips. I hand him the knife, hoping that the gentle gesture of his when he takes it isn't somehow sinister. "Don't choke up on the handle. Let the blade do the work."

"What are *you* going to do?" he wants to know.

"It's Christmas, right? We need a main dish."

Lo's attention seems to drop, gathering darkly among the familiar kitchen smells before he casts it through my kitchen window, out into the front yard where my chickens chuckle and dip for feed.

"Real meat," he says shyly. "It is a day of first principals after all. Isn't it, Cook?"

When I was a boy and had informed ©*Godmother* that my wish, finally, was to be a cook, one of her first Vocational Conviction Tests was to take me on a virtual tour of a slaughterhouse.

I'd cried through most of it, but I could still hear her whisper in my head that to cook was to kill. That the essence of flavor was really a reconciliation with ghosts.

I remember sitting there in my father's miasma of pot smoke while he blissfully chewed my first foray into stoner food: Oreos fried in bacon fat and drizzled with maple syrup and real bacon bits. He had smiled at me. Not even the vibrations of the ©*Pumpkin* implant in my little nine-year-old sinus thrilled me as much as that smile and I was convinced, right then and there, that only death would keep us satisfyingly fed.

Years later I equally remember arguing for my using meat with Carlos before my departure, dismissing his charges of "anachronistic cruelty" before being convinced by his more salient insistence on practicality.

Mars has no open pastures, no oceans teeming with briny main dishes.

It was hard enough to get him to sign off on Lily and a dozen nitrogen-suspended fertilized chicken eggs. And I guess I'm just too ruled by my own culinary first principals to go strictly vegan.

So, I compromised by relying on a repurposed medical tissue printer for my animal proteins. It's a pricy little bastard, Carlos has assured me, with mimetic carbon fidelity tipping at the quark level. But still, it could only print the singularity I'd fed it.

So, every Wagyu beef fillet was the *same* fillet, nurtured by the same local grasses grown by a single arcing season.

Every salmon steak, a clone pulled invariantly from the same cold Alaskan creek on the same single morning.

This was until I figured out how to hack into the spice jar of Wiloughby's memory files and make a name for myself.

But my memories are not as delicious as the rest of Wiloughby's. So, every Christmas, I secretly cull a slowing producer from my laying flock and treat myself.

"Let me do it," Lo says, turning to me. "Let me kill it."

I feel a slight chill even as I smile at his enthusiasm. It's useless to say he doesn't know how to kill something. All anyone needs for the task is the will to do it. And this kid is simply brimming with will.

"One stroke," I say, nodding toward the small, bearded axe that hangs with the rest of my antique cutlery. "You don't want it to suffer."

"I won't need that," he says, passing soundlessly through my back door.

I watch him through the kitchen window. The chickens are calm when he enters the yard. He reaches down and picks up a palmful of dirt. The birds twitch curiously, heads bobbing, cocking blazing eyes toward his bent form. I watch as he calmly picks the small grains of feed from the grainy, pink soil, and when he has a sufficient amount, he offers this to the flock.

Clucks ripple on the still air as they gather, ducking toward the food.

He hums something. A tune I don't recognize at first.

I get a furious chill when, through his low soothing lullaby, I recognize the last song Harlem ever danced to: Trilla's variation on the *Allure Cola* jingle.

He sits on the thinly grooved stump, rusted from years of chicken blood, and waits. Huge minutes pass as he hums the whole song. He offers an open hand to the yard. Most jerk mindlessly away. But one is tempted.

A fat speckled red whose tail glistens with a faint oily iridescence. He starts to hum again, the fluctuations of melody lulling the small avian brain. And when the bird lowers its head, Lo allows it a cycle of just three of its sharp pecks before his other hand drifts silently behind it. He lifts it gently to his lap, peppering soothing clicks among the whispered tune, stroking the creature until its eyes glaze with calm. He reaches slowly to his back pocket, careful not to break the soothing spell, and takes out a length of ribbon.

I recognize the ribbon as the bookmark from my entrance table, and I watch as he drapes it like a muffler around the bird's feathered throat.

The bird doesn't seem to notice. An enchantment has been cast.

It has agreed.

If there is tension in the ribbon, I cannot see it. It is by degrees, by slow paths, by a subtle, gentle, somehow longed for deepening down that the creature finally stops and lays unmoving, as if it had never moved, in the shallow canyon of the boy's lap.

He looks up. I see his eyes.

Is there mercy there or something unclean in them? Something obscenely raised to ceremony that would have been easier to accept if it had remained a chore?

Then I notice there is no pride in his stare.

It is too cold and unmoving to welcome even acknowledgment. But still there is something familiar in it, a weary triumph he inexplicably knows we share.

And for a moment I am doused with an icy and irrevocable respect for the boy.

Chapter 8

Lo watches me as I singe the feathers loose in boiling water, stares calmly as I pluck its steaming carcass like weeds from a vegetable bed. When it comes time to gut the bird, I can feel him wince, slightly, sympathetic as the slit in the creature's belly reveals its shiny cache of innards to my waiting bowl.

"What will you do with that?" he asks, looking at the cooling muck.

"The livers are good fried. The blood might find its way into sausage or to thicken soup."

"What about the bones and the rest?"

"Stock. Nothing is wasted."

"Just the feathers," he says quietly.

"Too sharp for pillows," I say. "Could reduce them in the sonic enclave for glue but that reeks like hell."

"May I keep them?"

"What for?"

"May I?"

I am too curious to refuse him.

He watches my every move as I dice the carrots and onions I will use as a braising bed for the meat. I salt and pepper the chicken. Nothing else is needed. I pop the bird into the enclave, coaxing it to braising frequency. He stares at only my hands, in total silence as I prepare the rest of the meal.

Lo enjoys his Christmas dinner.

Or perhaps enjoy is too mild a term. He absorbs it with a reverence that is more unsettling than complimentary.

I start with a small *amuse bouche*, just the meager livers flash-fried and smothered with a brown butter reduction and black truffle. I've steamed a few dandelion greens and flecks of baby kale with roasted grapes and reduced balsamic and made a pan-baked corn bread with a crust of printed bacon fat and white meal. Pretty standard for the holiday. He comments on the faint petrol aftertaste of the printed bacon. He suggests I dial up the pH on the grapes to improve the color and tartness.

But the bird. The blood-funk that imbues only things with faces. The way its meat leaves the bone in savory bundles receives no prescriptive critique from him.

I have lost my appetite.

That the main dish we enjoy once lived is what we try to forget when we eat.

But this is precisely what the boy seems to relish.

The full arc. The whole cycle.

The honesty of his relish sickens me.

His favorite, as with all chicken connoisseurs, is the back, the little nuggets of muscle at the spinal joint of the wings, the oysters, that seem to house everything worth experiencing about the braised creature.

And as I watch him enjoy the food in reverential stillness, my mind keeps going back to the ribbon. The ribbon he took from the entrance table *before* he even knew what was on the menu.

Does he have a thing for pale blue satin?

Was he planning on garroting his balls before bed in some pain principal masturbation session like Anthony Bourdain was famous for doing when both his usual hookers and coke dealer refused his texts? Lo's owners are enough skin-jobbing sex freaks to have let something like that leak.

But somehow that doesn't seem right.

There's nothing so *ordinary* about this kid.

Then how the hell could he have anticipated the ribbon's use?

When we are finished, he asks about my restaurant. Since it's Christmas, I've carried the meal to The Church, letting the meat rest as we walk. I've set us up in the dining room proper, on a snow bound two-top of crisp, white linen and silver.

"It's quite beautiful in here," Lo says, looking at the empty tabletops and beadboard that lines the walls. "So simple. So, inviting."

"I was going for simple but classic. A little pre-corporate Keller. You know who that was?" I ask.

"Thomas Keller, *French Laundry,* Yountville California…" he chants like he knows it. He displays none of the idiot glaze the rest of us do when we ©*Godmother.* "Four stars, closed May of 2031…"

I should have ended up in that kitchen, a happy sous chef and would have if ©*Godmother* hadn't let go of the wheel after that morning in my mother's bedroom with the tree frogs singing and the sheets reddening.

"Well, I never got to eat there," I cut him off gently. "But I read his book. Cooked my way through it when I was about your age. Went to bed every night for a month repeating his mantra: *All eggs are large. All flour is all-purpose flour. Salt is always kosher. All pepper is freshly ground. All butter is unsalted. All herbs fresh...*" He mouths my words silently in time with mine. I slow as I notice.

"Shit," I say, not wanting to embarrass the boy. "I didn't bake a pie. You want a pie? I could print one. Cherry and quince?" He reaches into the bib of his overalls and takes out the gingerbread man I'd given him earlier. I never saw him take it.

"This will suffice," he says, biting off a brittle arm. Chewing, he reaches into a pocket on the leg of his overalls. "I was told to give you this." He removes a small device, no bigger and not much different than what we once used to remotely lock a car door. I take it.

"What is it?"

"My remote."

"Don't you just sleep on your own?"

"I don't sleep."

"*Ever?*"

"No. The beta frequency won't let me move but I don't—"

"That's horrible, Lo. That's fucking *awful.*"

"Is it?"

I don't know what to say. I didn't prepare a Shelf for the kid, couldn't stomach the thought.

I'm outraged by how he has been treated but still I can hardly imagine getting any sleep with him creeping around the house all night.

He looks at me, shifting his weight slightly, awaiting my assessment.

The empty restaurant floor creaks in the silence.

"I notice the compression rates of your floorboards here are not modulated," he says. "I noticed the same thing at your house. The creaking might keep you awake. I could stay outside." I'm relieved by his offer, but I can't let it pass.

"Like a dog?"

"Like the chickens. And your goat."

At the mention of Lily, my spine shoots cold darts to the base of my skull. Lily is my special pride. My glorious headwater of non-synth cream, milk, butter, and cheese. She had been specifically spliced with just enough bovine DNA to mellow her native funk while still maintaining that elusive savor without which I would still be dreaming about decent dairy. I raised her from a kid on gallons of her mother's cryo-extracted milk.

I sang to her.

I read to her.

I massaged her goaty little haunches an hour a day, every day, on my eighteen-month journey up here. I keep her printed alfalfa and poly-hydrated oats in a special temperature-controlled shed behind a veil of lemon grass back at my house. Out of eye and earshot. So how had he known about her?

"Why is your restaurant called *The Church of Buzz Aldrin*?" is all he offers to my unarticulated question. My irrational but visceral fear.

"That? Oh. Do you know what the first formal meal off-world was?" He blinks. Of course, he knows. He searched it while the question was still tumbling past my teeth. But he says nothing. For some reason he wants me to tell it. "The first moon landing," I say, sipping my wine. "A communion wafer and a shot of chianti. That's right. Buzz Aldrin was a Catholic. Bread and wine. So, it just seemed fitting."

"Do you miss Earth?" he asks. Does anyone miss their own infamy? The cold stares that met every job application after my release? The best I could get was dishwasher. Watching through the mirage heat of my dry sterilization station how the sous chefs cubed onions? That meticulous clatter of their knives that freed flavor better than any Cuban beat? Taking notes in the best kitchens of California, leaning on the handles of my vibrating mops?

I want to stay positive. If that fails, I at least want to stay on the topic of good food.

"I miss real marrow butter. Grass-fed veal shanks. Probably kill for a rasher of actual applewood smoked bacon and a few oxtails." How the hell I can think so lovingly about meat after our meal I don't know. I change gears. "I have rather embarrassing dreams about the plumpness of vine-ripened tomatoes. And I miss cooking with predictable blue flame. But Earth? Not much."

"Why do you call your goat Lily?" The question is somehow too intimate and I have to get off the defensive. So, I change the subject to something he might still be coveting.

"Where did you get the coin?" I ask. The boy doesn't even flinch. His sudden calm and knowing smile belies a mastery of the quid pro quo of delicate conversation.

"The one I used on Harlem?" Do I hear pride in his voice? Or a subverted remorse for my benefit.

"Yeah."

"It was a tip. From one of my owner's guests. A 1922 Liberty head. A real antique." *Was* I expecting evident remorse? I don't know. I'm only sorry I asked the question. But the boy keeps talking. "Do you know the last words of John Wilkes Booth?" he asks.

"No."

"*Useless. Useless,*" he was supposed to have said. And that's what the coin was. At least here on Wiloughby. At least until I gave it meaning." The evening is begging to end. But I won't let it. I am entranced. Like the bird the boy enjoyed. I have to know.

"How did you give it meaning, Lo?" I say measuredly.

"I turned it into a key." His eyes glow with his admission.

"What kind of key."

"A key for a music box," the boy says.

That's what Harlem was to him. Music trapped in a box of supple skin. He just had to know how it worked.

"And did you hear it, Lo? Did you hear Harlem's music?" The boy's eyes are bright with tears when he looks up at me. The deep brown of them blurs as they brim with what I can only read as gratitude.

"Cook," he whispers, "it heard *me*."

A BOY NAMED SOUS

Chapter 9

I didn't sleep that first night.

Not soundly.

I'd startle into the confused pixels of the red night, thinking I was hearing Lily's distinctive bleat while Lo spun a blue ribbon around her throat and began to hum Harlem's last jingle.

It's true I had the beta remote. I'd tossed it among the socks and relics of my top dresser drawer, hoping to lose it, to never be tempted to use it. And so, each hour, as I drifted off only to violently rouse myself into a houseful of darkness and silence, I weighed the insurance gained by paralyzing the boy, perhaps in mid-sentence, mid-thought, against those eyes that might reproach me for my selfish caution the next morning.

I wake to the smell of bacon. But not just any bacon.

That bacon. That final Sunday morning bacon when I am still a boy and the Los Angeles sunshine spilling through the skylights still held the simplest promise of breakfast and my father stood over a fussing skillet, taut and tan and handsome, slapping the hot grease from his bare shoulders and my mother's body sleeping for the last time upstairs, only

I didn't know that yet, and my father will have something to ask me.

I've never been able to synthesize bacon, not with this level of fidelity. I'd never bothered to sample a memory file of bacon and my improvisation on the bacon theme was off key, as Lo had informed me at Christmas dinner.

Perfect flavor projections are like death house blues, forbidden music passed on from ear alone.

How the hell had Lo learned the tune?

I slip on my old Beacon robe, the one I scanned from a 1920s Sears catalogue, guessing at the colors, and pad down the stairs.

The boy has been busy.

Seated at the kitchen table like the honored guest at some satanic soiree, is Lily, my goat. Her white fur has been combed. Around the roots of her horns, streaming past her thick neck, is a warbonnet of intricately woven red chicken feathers.

I am too shocked to smile.

Before her is a bowl of steaming alfalfa and oats. She looks at me with her loveless eyes, her jaw working up a green froth.

"Did you know lightly steaming the oats releases the estrogen? Means more milk, Cook. Her lactating capability is still greatly reduced due to the feed you have her on." He has a flour sack towel pinned around his waist. "Give me a minute. You like this stuff crisp, right?" he says turning the frying strips with a fork. No good morning. No respectful pre-coffee silence. Just the smell of frying bacon that reminds me of the worst morning of my life. And my goat. My precious, hidden goat the boy is not supposed to know about.

"How did she get out of her pen?"

It's all happiness in my kitchen.

The boy is happy.

The goat is happy.

The smells are happy.

But I can't be part of it.

I'm struggling with what feels like a violation and looks like a blessing. The specificity of the bacon would have been conversation enough but with my girl, my Lily in the mix I can't help but think this is how Lo has planned it. He wants me off balance, awed and horrified in equal measure.

"I'm sorry," he says, placing his fork near the skillet. "She was hungry and I thought you might be hungry and I just wanted to surprise you. Both of you. I'm sorry. Are you angry?" His explanation is logical, the dejection on his face enough to make me swallow my paranoia but not enough to stop me from feeling like a real shit.

"No, I'm sorry," I say, sitting down at the table. "She looks great. You need to show me the file you used for the bacon." I watch him head back into the kitchen. I sit and stroke Lily's boney head. "Look at you, girl. You good?"

Her powerful jaw muscles jump beneath my hand as Lo comes away from the skillet with a plate of evenly crinkled strips. He's gotten everything right but the color. The bacon is orange, or rather, in its denatured state, an odd shade of ochre. I'm not sure if I should tell him.

"I got the color wrong," he says, setting the plate down before me. I hold a strip to my face and bite. It is the taste of my last moment of bliss before my father takes me upstairs and changes everything.

"It's exactly how I remember it."

I look at the boy. He doesn't look at me. "How'd you do it?"

Lily's bowl is empty. Lo takes it, his voice trailing behind him as he heads toward the cupboards.

"You've been using a two-tiered glycoprotein in your slurry base. I doubled the matrix and pre-printed the individual components separately. With the stock file you created you can't really lean toward a variance."

"You *improvised* this? I don't understand. What did you use for reference?"

The boy's eyes are large, pupils as black as the irises, but even with all that surface area I cannot detect a single recognizable emotion.

"You don't have to eat it," he says quietly. He moves to clear the plate. I stop him.

"Hey, I'm impressed. *Really*. It took me forever to figure out how to freestyle with that fucking tissue printer." This is what he needs to hear. The confidence bleeds back into his face. "This needs eggs," I say. "Shirred with a melted gouda and a sourdough back." Anxiety ascends and disperses in his unblinking eyes before me. Does he need to hear more? "How'd you like to work for me, Lo? I mean at The Church?"

The boy is quiet. The only sound in the slanted rose light of the morning is the goat as she chews.

"How could I work for you? You're afraid to give me knives." His keen assessment of the situation is as refreshing as it its unnerving.

"I never said that." This is only technically true and so categorically false. I'm a little ashamed at so flimsy a defense. "I did it anyway, didn't I?"

His head is shied at a slightly deflective angle, as if my answers could somehow penetrate his statements and hurt him.

"You thought I'd hurt your goat," he says blankly.

How did you know that? I don't say.

"I like that goat."

How did you know that, Lo?

The boy has an answer but he will not give it.

He follows me to the stove where I crack eggs for baking into two glass ramekins. I'm confused at my function here. What had Carlos expected? That I reprimand the boy? Make him feel bad for Harlem and my own fears? Hold him responsible for actions that are clearly so outside his capacity of conscience that any correction on my part would seem arbitrary? What the boy needs is encouragement. Care. Precisely what I needed when I had been accused of something I might have wished for but didn't remember doing. I put my hand on his thin shoulder. He quakes so violently I am tempted to pull him into a hug. I look firmly into both of his eyes instead.

"I love that you like Lily, Lo." I smile at my accidental alliteration. "Lily Lo," I chuckle/smile. His eyes blush young again. And something in them lets me know he understands what his being here is becoming for me.

Or does he?

"If you really loved that goat like you say you'd change her feed. She's a ruminate after all."

"I know that. And her alfalfa slurry is cut with all the nutrients she needs."

"She needs grass."

"I understand that."

"She's lactating at probably a third of her capacity. She should be grazing."

"Get the gouda, will you?"

"You should print some grass for her, Cook," Lo says, grating the cheese on its finest setting and letting it sift evenly from the tips of his fingers onto the expectant yolks.

"Can't. You can't print grass."

"Why not?" Lo asks.

I slice the bread, calibrate for the best browning friction, somewhere between a moan and a cry if I could actually hear it and place the raw slices on the enclave's stainless grid.

"Same reason I can't print you a match that lights or a semi-automatic. It's forbidden. Built Water Allotments, even here on Wiloughby, won't allow for anything as decadent as grazing grass." Trilla could play for rain, she could get it to grow. But Trilla's talents are strictly proprietary.

"What about rye or barley seed," the boy wants to know. "You could grow grass with that. You could say you were baking a seed loaf."

"Both print sterile."

"But it will print alfalfa?"

"Only desiccated. Only hay. Hence the nutrient enhancements."

"Wheat? You could say you need the grass for juicing."

"It prints chlorophyll tablets. Same with sorghum, durum, spelt, kamut, amaranth, quinoa, hanza, sesame, chia, and flax seed. All sterile. You really think I haven't tried this?" He doesn't waste a second in his retort.

"There's grass around the Water Builder's yard," Lo says flatly. I try to cover the sudden fear that grips me. I don't want Lily anywhere near those Water Builders or their yard.

"That shit's *purple* for chrissakes," I try to say as dismissively as possible.

"What color should it be?"

"Grass? Not purple. She wouldn't eat it. Watch those eggs," I say moving to the glass door of the enclave. "You don't want that cheese too brittle."

"The eggs can stand another ten seconds," he says, throwing a look to the bubbling mass in the enclave. He turns to me. "How do you know, Cook?"

"How do I know what?" I ask, removing our toast from the grid and smearing it with softened butter.

"How do you know Lily won't eat the grass around the Water Builder's yard? Have you tried?" I remove the eggs and plate them, fanning the toast around the heated sides of the baking dishes, grabbing two forks. Lo follows me to the kitchen table.

"Listen, Lo," I say sitting. "I am fully aware of Lily's status as a cud chewing herbivore just as I am aware that her diet is less than optimum—"

"So, let's bring her to the yard," he interrupts. I notice the boy is still standing while he pleads the goat's case.

"Sit down. Will you please sit down, Lo, and we can discuss this?" The boy sits, careful not to look me in the eye. "You have to respect that I am doing my absolute best for Lily. Just like you have to respect that I have my reasons for not wanting her anywhere near the Water Builder's yard."

"It's probably just a pigment variance," the boy says, fingering the crust of his toast.

"What?"

"The color of the grass. All the iron in the soil would be very—"

"Lo! Come on," I say, dropping my fork. I regret the shattering clank the utensil makes as soon as I hear it. "Eat your breakfast. Please. Don't worry about Lily. As long as she's near us she's fine." I watch as he sullenly tears a neat strip of his toast and stabs through the melted crust of a ripe egg.

"Why don't you just admit it, Cook," he says while chewing. "It's not the color of the grass you're afraid of at the builder's yard."

The boy is right. I don't fear the grass. The grass is just an opportunistic growth feeding off the accumulated moisture from the holding tank condenser coils, one of the few bits of fallout Wiloughby did not plan for.

Another few bits of this fallout, although I feel pretty embarrassed and elitist to admit it, are the Water Builders themselves.

Chapter 10

When you wash in it, gargle it, or piss in it, you forget that hydrogen and oxygen are extremely volatile elements in their raw atomic states. And so, to husband such potentially catastrophic molecules, you'd need someone comfortable around the fierce glamour of violence and death.

They might have been harpooners or dynamite setters in another age, but on Wiloughby all Water Builders could boast PhDs in atomic physics. They might look like scary meth-burnt janitors but each one had done time at privately funded particle colliders all over the world. And each one had matriculated through college campuses that were then known as much for their graduate programs as their political activism. Once relatively peaceful social movements had now all gone gonzo militant on the grounds of every ivy league school in the country. Trans-racial rights activists, Cis-reversion right activists, water conservation advocates, animal rights activists, AI rights activists. All had given up on consumer ransomware attacks and meta-compiled social media shaming to make their points.

Amped on the unassailable righteousness of their causes, even middle school campuses were highjacked into multi-cause headquarters. Violence had soared back on Earth while I was still a boy, leveled and ultimately become the distinguishing element of their commitment. It was simple: Just watch your birth-biased slurs, eat the right kind of corn, never raise a sharp implement to a first growth conifer, treat AI the way you'd treat yourself, and never, *ever* harm an animal.

I knew that the night my Dad and I went to Caitlyn Jenner's latest gubernatorial fundraiser. The night PETA paid us all a visit and punctuated the earnestness of their ethical intentions toward animals with the blunt end of baseball bats.

Everybody had been dressed to the nines that night of the fundraiser. Even me.

So how the hell had the blonde in the coyote bolero at our table missed the memo?

Ms. Jenner, now in her twentieth skin retread, was running for re-election as California Governor, promising property tax repeal and Western Unity and was holding a cozy $100k per plate soiree. My mother was desperate to maintain her conservative facade but was too swamped with code to go. And my father was tired of being "the prize pussy in pants," as he called it, and in a huff at my mother's cold insistence that he show his face, took me as his plus one. My parent's nightly fights were getting louder, wetter-sounding, and she was probably just happy to have some time alone to wrestle with her syntax errors in peace. Taking me as his plus one was his parting *fuck you*. I don't think my mom knew I had even left the house.

We were about a third of our way into our Thai-basil steamed blowfish when they came in. Two guys and what could have been a girl, greyhound thin, eyebrows and hair shorn to angry stubble, faces scarred by the ravages of Corp-Stig. They were all dressed in creaking vinyl jump suits and rubber gloves. The blonde in the coyote skin bolero had been vocal during the vapor course, rabid in her assertion that the "brown" aversion resonators at the neutrino Wall needed to be at least thirty percent louder at the San Diego border to be effective. Even I could feel she was nervous she had offended me. Did she think I was "pre-boarder" born? I was confused. Her dishwater gaze had lingered on me, then shot to my father who I saw shake his head before mumbling something about my mom being black. This seemed to calm her but only confused me further. Everyone in the room but my dad was my color, either from blending or amped melanin coding.

The jumpsuits had fanned through the crowd. Police helicopters were already thumping the roof of the venue and sirens were shrill on the streets. I was wondering why the blonde wall-lady next to me was wearing a shaggy coat that smelled like soup when her skull shattered with a wet pink pop. I remember the hard chime her chopsticks made as they fell to the lip of her plate. Her three assailants kept up the steady hail of their wooden bats, coaxing every frequency of plosive and crack from her leaking frame, shouting "*they have feelings*!" and "*that skin once had a heartbeat!*" as the crowd around us screamed far less coherently. Their message sent, one of the attackers, slimmer than the others, grinned at me, so shellacked with gore I couldn't help my Fangoria stare. She hooked her finger in a crooked "p" to her chin before she and the other two of her soon-to-be martyred crew were shredded into hollow-point pulp by the cops.

So yes, the fact that a few of Wiloughby's Water Builders were still members of PETA freaked me out. Not for my sake. Or Lo's. Clearly, he could carve up all the lithe, lyrically gesticulating Builds he wanted to up there at the yard without so much as a peep from them. But bring Lily up there? After I had "co-opted her empirically autonomous physiology for my own recreational and hatefully bipedal culinary preferences?" That was never going to happen. Grazing her was out of the question if I wanted to keep her safe.

Lo looked at me and smiled.

"What?" I asked.

"Can we at least print a different butter churn, then?" He asks, biting into his toast and swallowing with what looks like some difficulty. "That eighteenth-century Dutch churn you have has only two paddles and the Norwegian pine is a little too resinous to not flavor the butter." I can't stop myself from smiling.

"Did you have a model in mind?"

Chapter 11

Lo began his apprenticeship with me in the dirt.

Or rather in the chemicals, as hydroponics were my agricultural default.

Having grown up on the shriveling soil of the Los Angeles Basin, where turf was as ostentatious as gold teeth, I had been taught to have a thing against lawns. It had gotten to where I didn't recognize a plant without its fringe of spectral roots, misted with nutrients, dangling from its growing cradle. But Lo appealed to first principals as well as my vanity, arguing what self-respecting antebellum farmhouse would be complete without a real planted garden?

If the Martian soil held a memory of fertility, it was tucked deep into the strata, flattened and frail like a flower pressed in an old, trashy novel.

The Martian soil simply needed to remember romance.

"There is nothing wrong with hydroponics," I had tried to argue my case with Lo.

"No. Nothing. Unless you want your carrots to taste like something *other* than rubber."

"But I've got all these misting cradles already set up." I was whining. I could hear myself whining.

"Afraid of a little hard work, Cook? Or is first principal flavor really not your thing after all?" You couldn't argue with the kid. And I was secretly happy our confrontational banter had taken on a more familial tone. We were bonding.

It was now my turn to watch Lo as he prepped what would be our garden beds. He collected Lily's solid waste along with mounds of chicken shit and this, slurried in baths of interconverted nitrogen, he assured me would be enough to revitalize the groggy brick dust that passed for our vegetable beds. And where had Lo gotten the nitrogen? It was a forbidden substance I couldn't print. I had only one guess. There was only one place he could get the gas. How chummy was Lo getting on his late-night runs at the Water Builder's yard while I slept? What else was he taking back with him along with those frosty green canisters of breathy N?

The science was simple, at least for him. And we spent weeks turning the soil, slacking it into a moist blood-colored humus.

I was wary the morning I saw our kale crop break the pink soil with its tender smile of leaf. Drought, like any trauma, breeds prejudice.

One of the few lawns I remember was a pitiful patch of shade mix and weeds just outside the entrance of the Los Angeles Zoo in Griffith Park. I had gone there with my dad to see the Korean mammoth. The cages were mostly empty by then, their exotic tenants either dead or re-patriated to their native homes to stud against extinction. Keeping domesticated animals had fallen out of vogue thanks to PETA's new militant efforts, and so stray pit bulls and labradoodles lounged on the plaster ice that was the polar bear's now-vacant cell. Tabby cats and pigmy pigs spooned comatose in sun-induced stupors on the mottled slabs of the monkey cages. Only the crows were free, waiting stooped and silent on the branches of long-dead sycamores, waiting for the next toy schnauzer to kick off.

But nobody was looking at the animal displays anyway.

They were all in a daze, locked behind their battlefield stares and loopy grins as they ©*Godmother*ed like mad their own private Kenyan safaris on the dual screens of their retinal vaults.

©*Godmother*-ing was still in beta way back then on Earth.

It took a while for us to heed the spirit voices in our own heads that announced the gate change of our spouse's arriving flight or to trust the pixies behind our eyes that whispered what year Joe Montana won the Super Bowl. But we acclimated. Learned how to make the subtle hijacking of our minds look natural.

There were those brief pauses we all suffered, like cute little aneurysms, before the conversation could resume its flow. But we got good at it. So good we forgot we even had such profound portals in our skulls at all.

"Why do they even bother coming, Dad?" I asked, gripping his hand, a hand he rarely let me hold in public. My father just laughed. He always just laughed. Whether it was a side effect of all the Marley Golds he smoked or a residual from his generation's love affair with irony, I never knew. He was pre-©*Godmother* vintage and so, unlike the rest of the blissfully unimaginative world, was used to smirking at unanswered prayers.

"Look at that poor fucker," he said, leaning down to me, pointing to a young mother who was vigorously rubbing a red and rising welt on her forehead after she had gone temporarily blind while trying to ©*Godmother* the difference between a bonobo and a chimp for her young daughter. "That stupid bitch just ran into that pole!" Her adolescent daughter, not much older than me, was crying, shaking her mother's shoulders. Her little face was looking around helplessly, terrified, while her mother tried to blink her vision back into real time. "Your mom says with the new upgrades the interface will be less disorienting. But I for one will miss the high comedy of all these ass-munching tech-junkies." He was still chuckling when he pulled me past the young girl's cries. I remember looking back. No one had stopped to help them.

The mammoth was a disappointment. It stood there like an enormous blonde rug, swaying drunkenly on its huge, reconstituted feet, its long pale ringlets only occasionally disturbed by the nitrogen misters that chugged loudly to give the poor creature a breath of an overdue ice age. The fur beneath its eyes was matted and dark with weeping. The tips of the huge sweep of its distinctive tusks had been hacked off. It looked all the world like some reject from a Sid and Marty Croft file. I wanted to leap over its badly frosted barrier and hug it. I wanted to scream at all the idiots gawping at it and then hug it again. I imagined gripping its ropey locks, a pissed off Rapunzel with no real ever after. I saw myself seated on the rugged saddle of the nape its neck. And then I would shout something in perfect Mammoth tongue and rip out of there. The two of us would trumpet in angry triumph as we knocked all those assholes over like dumb bowling pins with the hard elbows of its tusks.

The mammoth's enclosure was a hastily constructed approximation of a snowbound cave, complete with paleolithic drawings. Crappy plaster statues of what were supposed to be cavemen flanked the enclosure. They carried flint-tipped spears and wore stiff fur parkas and leggings. Altamira by way of Disney's Matterhorn.

"What's wrong with it, Dad? Is it sick? Why won't it move?"

"Everything's wrong with it, buddy," he said disgustedly. "He's got to be hotter than hell in this LA sun. Can you imagine sleeping for thirty thousand years and waking up to this shit?"

The moat around the beast was dry, filled with the husks of disposable cell phones and de-salinated water boxes. A few kids with fake prosthetic arms were making a game of chucking krill-flavored crackers at it while their parents stood there, sweating almost audibly, a few sneaking glances our way. Then a cracker grazed my dad's shoulder and a few of the parents began to snicker.

My dad had been recognized. Even in his street clothes he had been outed. That meant it was time to go.

My dad was not popular, not among the residents of the San Fernando Valley Authority. He was a water cop, a patrolman for the Department of Resource Enforcement. His uniform was a thinly officious pair of powder blue tennis shorts and a white polo with an embroidered shield on the chest. He conducted his duties from the seat of a white city-issued beach cruiser, pedaling along the fake turf that passed for suburban frontage.

He was the bad news, the cold front in cloud-colored clothes.

Twenty times a day he ticketed reverse-mortgage widows who had watered their gardenias too liberally. A miserable trickle in the lap of a zen-garden Buddha could cost you five hundred credits. He almost lost an ear when he broke up a ten-year-old's water slide party.

But my dad didn't care.

He didn't take the job for its miserable pay and constant derision. He liked being out-doors, staying aggressively tan, keeping his stomach flat and calves toned. God knows, with what my mother brought in with her tech, we didn't need the money.

"Cook?" Hearing my name, what passed for my name, brings me out of my memories. Lo is standing there in front of me, soil-stained to the elbows with the dark Martian red all of Wiloughby now associates with his arms. He's handing me a Mason jar of what looks like lemonade. The acidity/sucrose matrix smells perfect. "Are you okay? You're breathing funny." It is only then I can feel my heart thundering in my chest. The slight rasp of air as it leaves my nostrils.

"I'm good. Just thinking about my dad. Isn't that weird? I haven't thought about my dad in years." This isn't quite true. I've only had thoughts about my dad since Lo came to live with me. Lo's smile is one of comfort. But also confirmation. Like he wants me to remember. I take the jar from him, brushing the dried maroon mud from the lip before I take a sip.

"Wow," I say swallowing. "Guava?"

"Just a hint." The boy smiles. His first maybe genuine smile. "Darn, I thought I had you."

Chapter 12

That night at dinner, I'm the quiet one. Our dinner is a simple cassoulet from a post-Revolution Huguenot file I scrounged out of my archives. A feast of the persecuted seems pertinent somehow. I sip my atomic Burgundy but Lo seems wary of his. I'm sure he's never had a drink before. What would alcohol do to him? He watches me. Then picks up his wine glass and sniffs it.

"Such delicate fermentation."

"Just yeast and sugar," I say.

"And geographic strata and weather and time. And love."

"Love and labor."

"They are the same if you labor correctly. Don't you think?"

"I do." I try not to broadcast my pride too obviously when I say this. I take another sip, keeping my eyes on the boy, his hands that hold the glass, his lips that are parting slightly now.

It's like a Roman victory when he takes a small swallow. I watch the slight convulsion of his throat, the way his eyes close as his palate is soothed and excited all at once.

"Surprising," he says at last.

"What is?"

"That good food could ever exist without that."

I chuckle.

"Well, don't guzzle it. I'm sure you're a lightweight." But it is too late. What remains in his glass is down his throat. Everything but the sediment.

"Are you meant to taste the sweat of the man who made it?" he asks with his eyes watering. "The good years when the cumulus came in abundance and the peasants made love in the shade of heavy summer leaves?"

"I don't—"

"Was it wrong?" He asks suddenly. His change in subject is hard to navigate. I want to hear him. I need to hear whatever he has to say. But I can't help a slight crush of disappointment. What else did he taste in the printed vintage? He could probably tell me the year and season it was bottled. The names of the vintner's grandchildren. I shake it off. We have time. New Years is just around the corner.

"Was *what* wrong?"

"What happened to Harlem." What *happened* to Harlem. The phrasing is interesting. But from Lo it has to be intentional.

"*Happened* connotes an inevitability," I try to say casually.

"You don't believe in the cult of free will, do you?" He seems genuinely surprised.

"In the broader sense, no. But there is such a thing as intentionality. Choice."

"But how can you kill something that you know for certain will live again? How is what I did any different than picking a flower? Or pulling up a leaf of kale?" It's an argument that gave whatever is left of Post Modernism its teeth. Bequeathed folks like Sam Harris their own little bodhisattva status and public parks. Tech has always driven morality. Always moved the baseline. And I'm feeling my wine and wouldn't stand a chance engaging this kid in a heuristic debate.

"I think making things is important," I say, finally, sitting back and fingering the stem of my wine glass. "And making things from a deep sense of ourselves is most important. But whatever you think Harlem was or what I think or science thinks Harlem was does not change the fact that the Harlem that *was* only happened once. And she *ended* only once. "

"But she was just a Build." It is subtle but I can sense a hint of self-loathing in his voice. Or is this what he wants me to think?

"She was a *person*, Lo."

"You really believe that?"

"With all my heart." It is so quiet in my kitchen I swear I can hear the slight hush of the water that crests his left tear duct. He breathes deeply, thinking so hard the air around us now seems to hum.

"Then if I'm good, you will forgive me?"

"Look at me." I reach out and gently grab his hand. He tries to pull it way, a rabbit-quick move that almost eludes my grasp. But if I have one advantage over the boy, I am just that little bit stronger than he. "I don't *need* to forgive you. *You* don't even need to forgive you. Not now. Maybe never. All you need to do, Lo, is *grow*."

Chapter 13

That night I can't sleep. The air in my room is a perfect 68 degrees, just like it is every night in my house. But my Depression-era wedding quilt is stifling tonight. The bodiless crickets thrum through the rolled nineteenth-century glass of my mullioned windows. The pink glare of Mars' two moons is beautifully dulled by liquid shades in the glass. But there is no comfort here. No warm heft to the solid simulation of a home I never had.

My mind races.

All this talk of forgiveness and fatherly hand-holding, all these gestures of blood-closeness and care are only what I'd wished I'd heard and felt when I was a boy. Everything I give Lo is a flimsy wish against the onslaught of memories that harp at me now. Am I as fake as the food I serve? What is my true provenance if not pain? And why is that pain so feral tonight? Lo is quiet downstairs. I feel he has not left the house, but I know he is waiting for something. Sitting there in the dark, upright and alert on my printed horsehair sofa, feet firmly on my atomically perfect, totally neglected farmhouse floors. He is waiting. Waiting for me.

Waiting for me to dream.

My father never wanted my mother to wash before sex. It was one of the few stipulations left to him in his semi-kitsch role of resident piece of ass. He craved the accumulation of her friction, rooted for it like a fan in the stands, the salt and yeast that rimmed her skin in the progression of her day. He argued it made her taste more real, more human. But she knew he meant more flawed.

More like him.

So, my mother ignored him, preferring the printed jasmine that scented her sonic shower and the pre-nup she kept stored in her hard drive.

When they started hitting one another during their fights, washing, along with conjugal sex, lost all priority.

My mother was not especially smart or insightful. Of course, she was brilliant, almost preternaturally so in her ability to understand the functionality of complex systems completely free of bias.

She wasn't *self* smart.

Or maybe that was her greatest genius. That she never had a self that occluded her view of the world.

She was of average height, darker complected than average, with a plain but pleasant prettiness that reduced her to near invisibility. She eschewed weaves. Hated head scarves. She wore her hair natural, cropped close to her head. Her eyes might have been stunning. They were large and almond shaped, framed with lashes so long and curly she trimmed them to stubs when she remembered to. Her irises were the exact shade as her pupils and could have seduced anyone with their depth and clarity if her stare hadn't reminded them of an event horizon. She had a habit of looking through things, never at them. The surface of things was never enough for her gaze.

The one quality she possessed, the one countless journalists would years later struggle to imbue with the agency of her success, was an unquenchable desire to understand precisely what was expected and then do just that. She was special. But she knew seeming special made her a target.

A finely crafted semblance of mediocrity was my mother's legacy. The toxicity of dreams was her credo.

Her own mother worked behind a trolley, collecting spit samples ten hours a day for cheap gene sequencers. She set up in parking lots dotting various strip malls around greater Azusa. Her father was a body player for a streaming television studio in Van Nuys.

Every morning her mother corralled tubes of anonymous pearly froth while her husband, equally anonymous, slipped into a shockingly blue MoCap suit and puppeted himself through wide shots and close-ups that would later be CGIed with the animated incongruities of deceased leading men.

My mother graduated high school with a C+ average. She didn't go to her graduation ceremony. She stayed home that day and did a tireless Feed search of the most accepted college essay themes. She didn't want to be freighted with anyone's expectations.

She got accepted to a landlocked state institution better known for its STD awareness literature and beer bongs than for instructing the best and brightest. She attended her classes religiously, mastering the look of boredom she saw in the faces of the students around her. She went to the prescribed parties, sipping from her canned daiquiri, braying in perfectly feigned disappointment at her teacher's intractableness, her menstrual cramps, the latest shocking cast change on Real Husbands of Boulder Christian Consolidated.

Her construct of the unremarkable co-ed was humming along nicely until one spring semester. She thought she was attending an introductory lecture to Psych I. Then she realized she had stumbled into a graduate course on computer coding.

Everything changed.

The professor's drone was a lotus of wisdom unfurling suddenly in bright and oddly familiar colors. The vagaries of UNIX were simple hymns, revealed as if under the golden tablet of some American religion. Code seemed to flow from her fingertips like her brain had been born binary.

Within a month she had graduated to C++.

This newfound proclivity for software design terrified her. She was careful not to call it a talent. Talent would lift her up above the herd, set her upon the murky path where hope was not that thing with feathers. It was something you stepped in.

Then one day, something happened that she could not qualify or contain or crunch into zeros and ones. She fell in love.

While crossing the quad one unusually warm February day in her tastefully cropped state sweatshirt, she saw the blue-collar Adonis that was my father flex his external obliques while catching a frosty Shiner Bock in the net of his lacrosse stick. Just as some bees can mistake the pristine surface of a swimming pool for sky, my mother mistook my father's physical perfection as an evenly tanned reliquary coddling every male virtue. Confident he must figure into her plans, she shocked herself when she asked him out.

Possessing the one pair of matched chromosomes he had yet to see naked and coming off a stressful week where two of his conquests were on pregnancy watch, my father figured why the fuck not. He agreed to meet her at the school commissary where he sipped from a paper bag while she demurely sipped her Ambient Cola. She knew his reputation on campus. Even watching him get drunker and drunker in the commissary, she had been mentally counting out the admission price to claim him as her own. His coin of choice was the casual hook up. She was woefully shy of funds.

My mother panicked. How could she win this player's sandy blonde heart? She had little experience, had only been partially felt up her twelfth summer during a bargain matinee of the Channing Tatum, Lee Van Cleef remake of *Jaws*. Her date had been none other than DeShawn Ramirez, who later became the NVP point guard of the New England Democratic Socialist Federation's one national basketball team, The Bernies. DeShawn had been totally into her. But my mother was not looking to be anybody's trophy. She wanted a trophy of her own.

My father was hardly transformed by their time in bed. But he was intrigued. Her fumbling gratitude was a new kind of Viagra for him.

To keep him interested she let him hit her.

A slap on the ass, that first time, probably harder than she cared for, but enough to imprint the averageness of her naked body on his pot-slowed synapses. But that wasn't what my dad-to-be wanted.

He wanted to be hit.

He wanted to be hurt.

Her self-loathing was a well-constructed ruse. But my dad's was the real thing. He knew he was a piece of shit even then and he wanted to feel it. It took some coaxing. A few reams of duct tape and a studded ping pong paddle. But my mother finally got the hang of it. The night she chipped his canine with the butt of her straightening iron was the hottest experience of his young life.

Fairly soon, a strange thing began to happen to him. In the post-game shower, palm-slick before sleep, it was my mother's loopy grin, her unspectacular face, and average legs that coalesced out of the darkness before my father jacked off. He simply had to have her.

That next winter they were a standard campus item.

She composed his Comparative Biology midterm in a perfect simulacrum of his simple sentence staccato, played him vintage Stones when he had trouble remembering Pavlov for his Psych 1 midterm final.

He gave her her first teeth-rattling orgasm. She coaxed his GPA to just past passing so he wouldn't be dropped from the lacrosse team. They were an oddly perfect team. Even if he did cheat on her.

Undaunted when she finally realized he really was just a bubble-headed pussy-hound with a formidable six pack, she decided to make him her project. She stole his smartphone and ripped a simple voice prompt app that would whisper in Cardi B's vintage growl when to wake, what classes to attend, what questions to cram for, what courses he could safely ignore and still not make the dean's disciplinary list.

"This is bitchin'," he said one late Sunday morning, "like having your own personal fairy godmother. You should market this, babe." For a girl allergic to wishes, the suggestion was strangely revelatory.

One year before graduating, she announced she was dropping out. And since there was no future playing lacrosse, he dropped out with her. But she assured him he needn't worry. She had a plan that would keep the two of them in indefinite clover. She called her "plan" ©*Godmother*, in deference to my father's breezy assessment of her first beta version. My father toasted her filing of her first intellectual copyright with a jaw so tender it couldn't tolerate solid food.

Chapter 14

It wasn't long after the release of her OS that ©*Godmother* entered the Valhalla of all proprietary corporate tech by becoming a verb. ©*Godmother*-ing was what you did if you had even a cursory interest in touching the world beyond the solitary circumference of your own navel.

My father loafed in grand style before my mother forced him into some semblance of a job that wouldn't be too taxing but still offer a modicum of self-respect.

That's when he became a water cop.

And my mother became rumor, haunting the hallways of their Encino mansion on her way to pee between coding sessions, eating a few bites of holiday dinner before recusing herself back to pixelville. Not surprisingly, perhaps rhetorically, my mother's investors were not happy with just the soft center of global communications. They wanted the hard candy shell as well. External devices were outdated mules, her handlers reasoned, dropping their steaming vulnerabilities on the cold tarmac of the last century. They wanted something new, something seamless and internal. Something you couldn't steal or drop into one of the few pools that still dotted the country's wealthier suburbs. Something you could never switch off or forget or ever be without.

My mother was not the first to develop the bio-interface. But she may have been the first to orchestrate the greatest mass personal information hack in history. The only one to ensure her brand of the internal interface would be government mandated.

The silicone dons of both California valleys had tried for years to foist the bio-interface on the general population with no luck. Even when nanobots became the diagnostic default, people were still gun-shy. No one wanted tiny machines injected into their bloodstream let alone a graphene derivative device no bigger than a single grain of quinoa shoved up their nose just so they could check their social media status.

Then one morning, five hundred million people worldwide woke up to find everything from their social security numbers to their porn preferences floating like pollen in the murky abyss of the Deep Feed.

Two days later that number doubled.

And it kept going up until my mother was finally invited to an emergency session of the National Ways and Means Committee. ©*Pumpkin,* as she called her thematically cohesive sinus implant, was her solution. Or rather, her ransom for the billion-plus lives she had kidnapped.

From my mother's original patent application:

Once coded with specific mitochondrial receptors, the device merely has to be released in the same room before it lodges quietly behind the consumer's medial pterygoid plate and sets up shop, via a series of bio-mimetic conduits. Within fifteen minutes, the consumer's optic chasm and tympanic nerves have been breached, effectively hardwiring one to the world forever.

Maybe safety was her real motivation.

Maybe her investors had had a darker purpose. I only know that after a tsunami of private lawsuits, every asset she had was frozen—six days after her death went public.

I can also tell you safety was not on her mind when she "field tested" her first version of the ©*Pumpkin.*

It must say "software developer" somewhere on my birth certificate.

Do I remember the room? Of course. It was my mother's room. Even with her liquid pixel walls bleached of the dense tangle of rainforest she projected when she slept, even without the chirp of tree frogs and the smell of damp camphor and rot that soothed her nightly into oblivion, I knew it was her room.

Did I understand why the doors and windows were sealed shut with magnetic tape?

How could I?

I was five years old. My age was important because I had developed advanced verbal skills by that time and reliable data was paramount to my mother's success.

Did I know what was lurking in the air among the dust motes and the skunky smell of my father's cigarettes and the ozone outgassing of my mother's ever-throbbing hard drives in that room?

I was too busy playing with my new CAS-9 pterodactyl, having just fed it a particularly large chunk of kiwi-flavored gum and delighting in the frustrated whap of its tiny beak.

I remember one moment I was laughing, enjoying the thoughtless breathing of any engaged child, and the next moment feeling as if an ember of molten lava had veered into my right nostril. I remember it burned as I tried to sneeze it out, burning even more as my eyes began to water uncontrollably as it scorched the blackness above my hard palate. I remember my heart racing, my whole body sweating as the nausea began to surface in me as it forced its way into my senses.

I remember calling for my mom.

And calling for my mom. And calling for my mom as the smell of burnt bubblegum imploded inside my sinus.

I remember losing sight in my right eye while I screamed for her. Screaming some more when that sight came blinking back in a panicked blur of that familiar room.

I don't remember the seizure. The frothing at the mouth. Or the pounding of my father's fists on the bedroom door. Or the concussion that was the sound of my mother's small body being hurled against the opposite wall when my father finally kicked the door in to rescue me. I don't remember these things.

But ©*Godmother* does. Those sights and sounds were the first sensation files ©*Pumpkin* ever recorded.

I don't know if you actually love your parents when you are that young. A crude prehensile instinct of trust maybe holds the place for love until you are conscious enough to really understand it. So maybe that was the part of me that lost its grip on my feeling for my mother that day. I had become a commodity. And my father had by then settled beneath the cheap electroplate of his trophy status.

At least we were alike in our remote usefulness to her.

It's no puzzle, then, why my real comrade in exile was my dad. I was too precious as a test subject to risk playing with other kids. My dad would have to do as my playmate. He contrived cunning escapes from the proprietary eyes of my mother's household cameras. Foiling entire afternoons of tests and upgrade sessions with kill words cajoled from my mother when they'd had angry sex the night before.

He'd hand me a spoon, dropping with a grin to his knees and we'd pretend to tunnel out, down the stairs and through the front door to his hydrogen-celled '69 Nova, two Steve McQueens, huffing our new freedom as he laid serious rubber.

He always ended up in some launchpad bar chatting up an ex-shuttle attendant or in the dark of a jack-off cubical in Van Nuys while I waited for him with my pro-secessionist podcasts in the passenger seat.

But there was salted caramel gelato on LA's version of Broadway, the latest war games at the Million Dollar Theater to cool his guilt for having made me wait. And when all that failed, when the hour was too late for war games or gelato lost its native sweetness after ©*Godmother* one day declared lactose "dietarily insufficient," we still had the common currency that kept us flush: our hate for her.

And our pact that one day, when his virtual scratcher hit the Mega Billions or he hooked up with another sugar mama or I grew big and strong, we would storm the front gates of our luxury dungeon and slay our cyber jailer once and for all.

But I swear to God I don't remember killing her.

Chapter 15

Consistency and attention to detail make a good gardener. One is an inexhaustible midwife to the vacancies of seed cups. And Lo was nothing if not constant.

I have to admit he had worlds more stamina than I. And when it came time to lay in the main verge, the lettuces and cruciferous vegetables, I left him to his own devices. I'd watch him bend into the slant of the late afternoon, foreshortened to the abstraction of a boy, creeping along the reddish rows, whispering to plants he only knew as file images, as slow and formative as a continental drift.

Some days I'd sit on the porch and work on that week's menu, listening to my '78s on my solar-cranked phonograph. And while gut-bucket blues thinned across the dry alien air, I thought the shapes his mouth made were approximations of my record's lyrics, that he was chanting to himself along with Bessie Smith that *nobody loves you when you're down and out.*

But the sync was off. His words were too direct, too earnest. And when the needle stuck at the end of its play and allowed his words to reach me, I realized it was the seedlings he was talking to, the tender pale shoots with whom he seemed to be negotiating.

In the evenings he'd want answers. At least he'd ask questions. And I'd sit there over our dinner, working again the week's menu, my kitchen congested with the requested peculiarities of Wiloughby's elite: the toothpaste shade of green of the split pea soup the Dexter-Fleetwoods shared at a roadside flop just outside of Bishop the day they signed the ownership papers to the Owens Valley Water Authority; the precise murkiness of the perique-smoked reindeer tongues the Gruber-Lowensteins shared one midnight from a tin at the snowbound Reykjavik Shuttle Port. It was slow work, more sensorial calculus than actual cooking, but Lo kept peppering me with questions. Process did not interest him. He wondered about taste. About preference. About my myriad personal eccentricities. The first principals of me.

"Why do you listen to your music on that thing?" he might ask with a nod toward my phonograph. "The spindle holes on those disks are not perfectly centered and there's a pretty significant distortion. Don't you hear that?"

"Yeah, but that's a first pressing Bessie Smith, man. On the *O-keh* label. 1920. Before she blew up on Columbia. There's probably two of those left in the whole system."

"But she's off a whole octave. A digi-mix would correct for that."

"But then you'd only get the information. Not the *experience.*"

His dark eyes clouded. I felt a coolness starch the air. I had confused him.

"That doesn't make sense. It's still distorted."

"That's not distortion, that's flavor, the way *she* might have heard it. You understand?"

He shook his head, frigid wisps of anger stealing from his pupils.

"The experience is shared," I continued. "With the past. Not translated. Not an imitation. The real thing." And I got up and gently removed the disk from the worn green felt of the turntable. I held it in front of him, from the edges, blowing on it lightly, out of habit, out of respect.

"You see those grooves? That's one of the first straight to disk recordings. Those are actual little canyons of sound."

"I understand the analogue process," he said sharply.

"But what you don't understand is when this '78 was cut she was still alive. Still striving. Yearning. Still *healing* from her latest romantic disaster. And all that blues broth, all that living, was carved into this frail little wax face. With her in the next room. It is a witness to all that. You understand?"

He paused. I could sense him searching. Thousands of sites, thousands of kilometers of conflicting code.

"Let me show you," I said finally.

He followed me to the front room and sat on the couch. Behind the worn beadboard next to my hearth I keep a wall-sized tryptamine pixel screen. It's a pretty snazzy setup with full immersion capabilities. I only use it when I can't bear to crack one of my first editions again or loneliness full-nelson's my imagination to the ground and I need a comfort or a release the waking world could never provide. I select for "ghost mode" on the experience remote. No need to interact with what our senses will tell us is real.

I ©*Godmother* a link to the main console and select the particulars, and slowly my room on Mars plumes with the smells of a sepia-toned and archived Earth. Dust and distance and beer-spilled hardwood floors. Cigarettes and pomade. Human sweat. Brass polish and the faint honey sweetness of an uncut recording disk. We hear the hard leather heels of two-toned shoes, the whiskey-flayed voices of the musicians as they prime their instruments. And there is the big woman herself, so real and solid in my front room I could touch her. Her thick neck and wrestler's arms straining the seams of her faded satin gown. I can smell the dusty softness of her body talc as her pit sweat bleeds deep rings at the sides of her dress. Stale corn liquor, sour cigarette smoke. But no fear. She fumbles the string of pearls she just bought with her first royalty advance. She spits on the floor, laughing as she rubs her crotch through the sheen of her dress. Her gown rustles as she adjusts her mountainous breasts.

"For luck, honey," she chortles before she steps to the fruit-wood flower of the recording cowl. She is so close to the flange she could kiss it.

She's so actual, so immediate, so ripe for greatness you could reach out and hug her.

It's a construct, of course. A best-guess cobbled together from documented prop and sensory files from all over the Feed.

I can feel the boy's impatience with the approximation, the lie that has me so thoroughly enthralled.

"But why does all that matter?" he blurts, breaking the spell of the past and my link with the screen. I take a moment before I look at him.

"Because we're human, Lo." His face is a blank, a mask of unformed assertions. "And there is a fidelity that I think transcends what we hear."

Then a spark. A crossing over a threshold to understanding.

"You mean like the chicken."

"The what?"

"The chicken we had that first night. Christmas dinner."

"Not everyone can taste the difference between the printed and the real. But it's there. And that recognition, that *deference* to the real, that's what makes it great."

"It's why you keep all these books."

"Precisely."

"Because the pulp is haunted." He gets it. Or at least I think he does. The pulp thing is a little fan boy for me. I'm thinking about more actively visceral experiences.

"More like the chicken," I say.

"Because of the essence."

"Exactly."

"Because of the *blood*."

Chapter 16

I remember standing on a similar edge of myself, years ago, when I was sitting in my room at the Calabasas Correctional Center. I had been ignoring the warden's wife after our furtive tryst in the facility's sauna, and I could feel my rejection of her, conflicted as it was, sharpening her attitude toward me. She had tried to win me back in the subtle ways at her disposal, but my fingers, knees, and eyes had quietly refused every one of her hidden advances.

It's not that I didn't want the body she was wearing or what she could do with it. God knows I was at an age when every other thought of mine had something to do with girls. It was the feeling of being imposed upon that bothered me. The intimate invasion of another's desires, no matter how tempting, that still held the guilt and shame I'd felt when my mother had used me to test her ©*Pumpkin*.

I'm making this all sound pretty glib. But in reality, it took me years of ©*Godmother*-ing gestalt files to finally get it straight in my head that I suffered from "a despondency resulting from an objectification identity brought on by 'technological trauma'."

Maybe this was another thing I shared with Lo.

I knew I was walking the line with the warden's wife, that my continued rebuff of her could lead to serious repercussions. She had the power to limit my privileges, confine me, or worse. Instead, she sent me a book. On the cover page she had written "which one are you?" I don't think I had ever held a paper book before then, let alone actually seen one. I was a child of the virtual age, where the only effort required of me was wishing. As I scanned the print and turned the pages, forced finally to be an accomplice in my growth and not just a passive recipient, a curious thing happened. I fell in love with not knowing. I fell in love with first principals. I fell in love with things that had nothing to do with my own projected self-interests. I still have the book. It was the only thing I'd taken with me upon my release that I had not had when I was detained.

"You ever hear of Hesse?" I ask Lo.

"Herman?"

"The same. Read *Narcissus and Goldmund.*"

The boy almost laughs. "Come on, Cook. I know the meme. The monk and the knight? Stock Freudian dualities of man in the form of a fable. It's corny."

"Sometimes corny is good." I search my shelves and hand him the book the warden's wife had given me all those years ago.

"What's the point?" he says, taking the book and placing it back on the shelf.

"Read it, Lo," I say earnestly. "And decide which one you are. A creature of the mind or a creature of the senses. Are you Narcissus? Or are you Goldmund?"

The next morning with my coffee he announces he is neither.

I notice the book has not left its place on my shelf.

"I am the rectory tree," he says, referring to the book's opening chapter. "And the tree does not need to decide."

The days were getting colder. In the mornings, there was frost on the young leaves of the garden Lo had planted. Wiloughby's air was thinning, becoming effaced and permeable to the frigid native weather of Mars. It was announced that even without Harlem, the launching of the atmosphere processors could no longer be delayed. It was hard to read Lo's face when I told him I thought we should go to the launching and the Build's recital that would follow. He was slow finishing his breakfast the day we were to attend it.

"It's just going to be Trilla and Isaac, right?" he said, smoothing the surface of his oatmeal with the back of his spoon.

"Trilla's composed a piece that will make the sunshine. Don't you want to see that?" He pushed his bowl away.

"I need to solar shroud the lettuces. I'm worried about the prismatic effects of the frost," he said.

"The frost will slow the growth and concentrate the flavor," I said.

"What about Lily then? She's still sluggish. She's barely producing." That was true. Ever since that first morning when Lo had campaigned for Lily's grazing, the goat had not quite been herself. I was worried, too, but not so much at her change in temperament. It was the timing of Lo's insistence, how his suggestion of grazing had coincided with her disinterest in her usual feed. I thought it best for all of us if Lo and I got out for a while.

"Come on. I'm sure Trilla and Isaac would want to see you. Don't you want to see your friends?"

"Friends" was a strong word. I'd known it as soon as I'd said it.

"Come on, Cook," he said shyly but without a trace of self-pity. "They're my phenotype. Not my friends."

The streets of Wiloughby are not paved. They're more paths, really, pink trails of decomposed native soil that I guess were left that way to mimic the decomposed granite paths of the more remote and exclusive spa communities back on Earth. You follow these paths past the elegant stems of the communication augmenting towers, past the small mercantile, an extruded replica of East Hampton's *Loaves and Fishes*, where you can purchase pheromone "candles" and tins of unprinted Beluga caviar—anything you don't feel like printing at home—to the large gravel circle where all the path's on Wiloughby converge. This is the Hub, the community consolidation center, although there is not much community and very little consolidating. It is here we assemble twice a year to watch the spectacle of the launch, take a deep communal breath of the freshly recharged air. It's where some go to flex their surrogate and expensive family pride.

Isaac has grown a model for the occasion. It is a three-foot mock-up of what is to be the new spa facility. He has designed it as an old stave church. I suppose in deference to Northern Europe's supremacy with body care and the denizens of Wiloughby's ecclesiastical appreciation of it. It's a magnificent thing, all raw mimetic timber, with support posts filigreed with intricate Celtic knotting and roof beams ending in curling dragon heads. It will house an infrared sauna and twelve circular tubs of coopered cedar. Each tub will be filled with Carlos Yakamura's special blend of amniotic fluid, the same stuff the Build's stew in before they are "born." Isaac assures the citizens that the fluid has a salinity that will allow for both perfect buoyancy and total relaxation.

The citizens are impressed but some want to know where the massage tables will go. Isaac smiles when he apologizes for not being clear. The fluid, like its organic uterine counterpart, is infused with heavy doses of oxytocin isotopes.

"Half an hour soaking in that stuff, you won't *need* a massage," he reassures us all.

I love the ripples in the model's wood grain, the fresh resinous smell of its cedar planks. But I wonder how it will ever render into real beauty without Trilla serenading the thing constantly and bringing the aging rain upon it.

His pitch ended, Isaac looks up to see Lo. He approaches the boy with a warm smile.

"Hey, brother," he says taking Lo's hand. "What's it look like? How you been?"

Lo will not look at him.

Isaac presses his lips together as his eyes soften. He pulls Lo to him and hugs him, whispering something into the boy's ear.

Lo smiles. Then he laughs. He looks up into Isaac's eyes, searching for some kind of confirmation and Isaac gives it. Whatever has passed between these two boys is completely lost on people not like them. Trilla scurries up and almost lifts Lo off the ground when she embraces him.

"Damn," she says, with her eyes still closed. "I thought I might have to come after you. I'm glad you came, baby."

Lo nods, looks the girl in the eye and another one of those silent moments he has just shared with Isaac passes between them.

Lo is demonstrably calmer when Trilla kisses him. She winks back at him as she goes to stand before her resonator board. It's an instrument I have never seen before. Probably something of her own invention. It looks to be a series of metal tubes, all with their hollows facing upward, housed in what looks like the ormolu body of a harpsichord. Everyone takes their seat. I notice Harlem's owners look at Lo then share a look between themselves. That shared look, whatever it has meant, sends a ripple through the rest of the seated assembly. A slight cooling that I can see disturbs the boy seated next to me. He has never been on this side of a recital before. He lowers his head, staring at the ground.

"Don't worry," I say squeezing his knee. "Just ignore them."

Trilla begins to play. I barely recognize her tune as a variation of Kurt Weil's "Lost in the Stars." Her rendition is stark, elegant, and nuanced, threading from major to minor keys with a fluidity and skill that leaves all our jaws slack and hearts perilously exposed.

Lo, the outsider is now in. At least the crowd has stopped staring at him.

The horizon begins to purple as the air scrubbers are released and the denuded ether becomes new again. The distance bleeds from purple to blue, to emerald green slowing into hues of yellow, orange, and red, thinning finally to a sultry and voluminous pink that undulates over our heads as Trilla ramps up her tempo.

Then comes the moment we all have been waiting for. The release of the solar enhancers.

The pink sky above us explodes and down comes a shimmering golden rain of refracted grains. The "sparks" are really helium launched solar-voltaic graphene reflectors, a kind of fool's gold, really, but so much brighter than last year's.

The air begins to warm. And soon the day is as promised: bright and sunny and calm. We can't help it. For that moment we are all identical in our happiness.

Even Lo is smiling.

That's why it takes me a moment to process what he says, to track the panic his face refuses to express.

"Did you lock Lily's pen?" he asks, grinning.

"What? Yeah. Of course. Why?" He's not smiling now.

"Something's not right," he says suddenly. "We have to go." Lo is standing before my eyes can process the compression of his knees. He threads his way through the seated crowd like quicksilver, disturbing no one. But the wake of derisive smirks and whispers he leaves in his wake are enough to capsize my composure. I stand and stiffly crab walk my way past the beautifully attired knees of all of Wiloughby, sensing the heavy confirmation of all their haughty assumptions. Clearly, I can't control the boy. Have taught him nothing of composure. I'm puffing out "sorry" and "excuse me" as fast as I can, hot shame heating my ears, my heart thumping with panic over the fate of my darling goat and the oily anger oozing from all those cold stares. I can hear a few of them begin a chorus of icy chuckles as I begin to run. The only cardio I've done in years has been in the form of chopping onions and butterflying printed Peking ducks. I'm chugging along gravel paths that have only known leisure. My short breaths are a sour note in the chronically calm sea air I designed myself. Lo is nowhere in sight. I scream his name as I pass an extruded version of Gaudi's Casa Vincens. I blaze in slow motion past a squatty reproduction of 10050 Ceilo Drive a famous crime writer shares with her partner. In my brain-shunting denial the only thought I can recognize is asking myself why Wiloughby doesn't have any trees.

When I get back to my house, I jog to the backyard, tearing my way through the growth that hides Lily's pen. I can see the gate to the pen is open as I approach.

"Lily?" I call into the quiet summer day. "Lily, girl?"

I check her pen.

It is empty, her feed untouched.

I run into the house, hearing my footfalls and breathing both heavy beneath me as I search the rooms. The comforting smells of earthy herbs and line-dried cotton mock my fear.

Neither the boy nor the goat is there.

"Lily? *Lo?*"

Then it hits me. There is only one place the boy and the goat could be.

Chapter 17

It's a scene that might look pastoral, but the colors are all wrong: a white goat laconically chewing purple grass under an orange sky. And the setting isn't a peasant's field or a distant windmill. It is the massive tanks of the Water Builder's yard. The last place I wanted to find her. My heart thunders in the calm hum of the holding tanks.

"Lily!" I call out.

The goat does not lift its head.

It is then I notice Lo, perhaps a yard from the goat, paralyzed as if he's afraid to move. He's staring at something and it's not the feeding goat. I follow his gaze and I see it.

I see them.

Three distinct shapes, standing by the foot of the holding tanks. Three distinct shapes whose details and intent the clarity of the newly scrubbed air cannot hide.

Water Builders. Hostility radiates off them like an animal's musk.

They wear pale blue coveralls the same color as Lo's. The same color as all service personnel on Wiloughby.

The air seems to magnify their features and even from my distance, perhaps six meters, I can see their shaved heads, their glass teeth implants as they smile at us. One turns to another and gestures and I can see where triangular windows have been cut into her face just below the cheekbones, giving me a full view, even through her closed mouth, of her clenched rows of frosted and brittle-looking molars.

They move toward us slowly, almost luxuriously, in a group, smiling as they approach. On their exposed forearms and on the tops of their chests and necks are the thick and angry looking welts of Corp-Stig.

Corporate-Stigmata Syndrome we called it back on Earth.

These builders might have been terrifying to look at, might have been highly skilled molecular technicians forced into blue-collar jobs. But they were all just deluded consumers at heart.

When my mother had made the ©*Godmother* platform impervious to advertising, Madison Avenue responded by turning the most frequent users of their products into human billboards. Trace elements of a modified rotavirus are what did it. Phase one attacked boneless tissue like the tongue, but with a few more years of heavy usage of your favorite brands, you would be scarred with corporate logos for life.

Within just months of its beta release, Corp-Stig outran traditional tattooing a hundred to one. I'd seen some pretty amazing designs on the shirtless losers trolling the Venice boardwalk when I was a boy. Tramp stamps of cartoon shrimp in full Tarantino jujitsu extolling the virtues of *Yume's Krill Krackers*. Full back pieces of demonic squids inviting gawkers to try *Ito's Black Ink Toast Treats*. The infected were surely proud of their corporate affiliations. That was until a few strains went retro and kids started dying from quaint little scourges like smallpox. Then it became a kind of Russian roulette only the most hardcore consumers could play.

The Water Builders stop equidistant between Lily and Lo and flash a series of quick gestures to one another. My heart stops as I recognize what they are communicating.

"Hey!" I shout. Lo holds up a quick hand to stop me.

"Don't, Cook," Lo says.

I can see the *Ambient Cola* logo emblazoned on their chests in pale pink scabs, the cola's catchphrase of "The Better Side of Down" snaking up their throats to the cliffs of their jawlines. One of them opens his mouth and I catch a glimpse of the denuded stump of his tongue. I mistake the sound he makes as a dry brand of laughter at first.

Then he makes it again and I realize he's bleating.

Bleating like a goat.

Lily lifts her head suddenly. She turns toward the sound.

"Lily!" I shout.

"Cook!" Lo shouts back. "Don't. Go home!"

The Builder bleats again as the three begin their slow trek backward toward the holding tanks.

"What? No, *Lily*!"

Lily shakes her head, the tremor echoing through her whole body. Then she bleats and begins to move toward the Builders and starts to follow them.

"*Lily*!"

"Cook! Goddamn it! Go! Go home!"

Was it then I saw the black carbide knives in the Builder's hands?

Or had they been holding them all along? I feint toward the retreating Builders

"Trust me, Cook. Please," Lo says, never breaking eye contact with them as they and the goat move farther up the hill toward the tanks. "Just trust me."

"Lo, no," I say weakly.

"*Go!*" Lo shouts with enough fury to make the Builder's jump slightly with surprise.

Something engages in me, some adamant motion in my hips and knees that turns me and sets me moving. Is it against my will or is the wisdom of his confidence and admonition beginning to inform me? I don't know. I'm too pissed and terrified, too helpless to tell.

I'm not fluent in the sign language of the Water Builders. But vaguely sharing the same service strata here on Wiloughby as they, I've picked up a few phrases. Enough to know two phrases they had used.

Milk Murderer and *Good Home.*

Chapter 18

Isaac and Trilla are sitting on my porch when I finally make it home. My head has been exploding with dread the whole way. They say nothing when they see me, just rise together as I fumble with the code to my front door and put their hands on me.

Their touch is like flipping a switch, like opening some hidden release valve and I am sobbing in the sloppy tripod of all our pressed together bodies, feeling my tears re-warmed and returned to me on their wet cheeks.

"Hey, Cookie. It's okay," Isaac purrs.

"Let me get you some valerian tea," Trilla suggests.

"I don't want tea," I say, as we all stagger through my doorway.

"You will."

Later, we are all seated at my kitchen table, a cup of hot tea releasing its uric stink in steam that teases my nose, but has gone untouched.

"You have to trust him, Cook," Trilla says, laying one of her enormous hands on mine. It feels as big as a blanket, warm and dry and comforting. "Drink your tea." I sip it absently, not asking how they know what's happening, not even caring. I'm just grateful I am not alone to grate my nerves over my worry and wonder.

I know I had locked her pen before we left. I can't help the nagging suspicion that Lo had let her out.

He's wanted the goat to graze.

He had not heeded my warning about the consequences.

"I checked Lily's pen, Cook," Isaac says. "The security code had not been upgraded so it just went into unlocking default."

Had that been the problem? Had I just been so buried with menus and work and the garden and the newness of the boy that I had just tabled something as important as upgrading her pen's code? I had to admit it was possible.

Just like it was possible I would never see Lily again.

And Lo was now disassembled, however inartistically, on the grass of the Water Builder's yard.

"Don't worry," Isaac smiles. "I upgraded the lock. She'll be safe and sound when she gets back."

"How can you be sure she's *coming* back?" I want to know.

"Because Lo is the best of us, Cook," Trilla says. "Although, even he doesn't know that yet."

Now it's my turn to ask questions, to seek answers to some if not all of my nagging suspicions. I get how Lo knows what he knows. He's doing it the same way all of us are. He's ©*Godmother*-ing.

I've also seen how the Builds, Trilla, Isaac, and Lo, are somehow connected, how they can share thoughts and soothe one another seemingly without words. The Builds are beautiful creatures, precocious not just in their creativity and caring but also in their innocence. The best in them would not allow them to see the worst in others.

They don't know the Water Builders like I do.

I know the open pen is my fault.

What I don't know is if Lo had somehow planted the idea of grazing into the creature's head. Was Lo capable of that? How else could I explain her leaving her pen, something she had never done before in all my years with her? Should I have used his beta remote on him? Could that have prevented all of this from happening? But if I'm seeking answers, I first have to reconcile myself to the falsity of my assumptions.

Lo is not ©*Godmother*ed.

Isaac tells me as much. None of the Builds are, they tell me. What would be the point of infusing them with the tech they exist to countermand? I say I don't understand. Trilla is gentle when she speaks to me.

"Your Mom's app is just another information system," she says to me, holding my damp hand. "Just another way to align oneself with potentially beneficial circumstances."

"We three are *informed* by our genetic prompts," Isaac tells me, "but we are strictly creatures of *lived* experience, Cook. Our truth is narrow, specific to what we think and feel and do." In other words, genuine artists.

"And what about Lo," I ask. "What's informing him?"

It is then they tell me the beta remote was never designed as an option for their owners. The remote is an option the Builds choose themselves. And only Lo has elected to use it. I want to know why. They are vague as to the boy's possible reasons. But I am left with the feeling that it has something to do with what is brewing in him, something deep and powerful and frightening that not even he can understand.

Something deep and powerful and frightening, like hacking into the simple mind of my goat because he'd believed grazing was best for her.

Just like I'd thought not using the remote was best for him.

"Are you saying I was stupid *not* to use it? That his beta remote is really a blessing?" I ask.

"A sort of blessing," Isaac answers. "An imperfect blessing." But also a crude one, I think to myself. An inelegant solution not in keeping with Carlos Yakamura's usual grace. So why is it there? To be used?

Or is it meant to be *overcome*?

The tea is making me sleepy. Or maybe the Build's themselves are doing it. Again, I can't tell. But as the hours pass, we become more and more quiet. It's a comfortable quiet. The kind of quiet mothers and fathers might bestow upon their children after hot and fervent days, the kind of quiet I have only read about and sometimes dreamed.

The quiet deepens.

It fills me up.

I don't feel the Builds anymore.

Or see them or hear them.

I am in the Water Builder's yard. A strange sort of picnic is taking place, one to which I have not been invited.

A working-class parody of Manet's *Déjeuner Sur L'herbe*.

The Water Builders are reclined on the purple grass, the elegance of their academic poses only slightly mocked by the filthy pale blue jumpsuits they wear. Lily is seated with them, her crooked legs knotted beneath her upright body, making her posture disturbingly human. She wears a pale blue jumpsuit too. The blonde female Water Builder is in the foreground, inexplicably nude like in Manet's original. Her pale body is embroidered, head to foot, with the red angry lace of Corp-Stig. They ignore me as they eat their lunch, a lunch that consists entirely of pulled purple grass. Their mouths are wine-red with it as they laugh drunkenly. Lily laughs with them. A human sort of laugh. The Water Builders pull hanks of the grass and begin stuffing it into Lily's mouth. Then their own. They pull more and more, oblivious to the clods of pink dirt that cling to the roots that are stuffed into their faces, shattering their glass teeth amid all that sickening burgundy drool as they continue to chew the dirt, the shards of their teeth and the peals of their own demented laughter.

Chapter 19

I wake to a hot grassy breath on my face. I am looking into Lily's loveless eyes. My whole body hurts from sleeping on my couch and it takes me a moment to break free from my dream. I throw my arms around her sinewy neck and weep.

"Hey, Cook."

Lo looks exhausted. Maybe a little disheveled as he sits calmly in one of the front room's easy chairs.

"Jesus," I say, sitting up. "How did you do it? How did you get her back?"

"That's not important," the boy says with a soft but eerie finality. "What's important is she's back and she's fine. And I'm sorry. I should have checked her pen code. It's my fault."

"No, hey," I say, reaching out to the boy. "It's not your fault. You didn't know." He's stiff when I hug him. But I won't let go. And I feel I'm tunneling, mining deep into him through hard strata and shale, all the impacted resistance he's built up over the years. Slowly he breaks and, like a newly dug well whose earthy bottom has finally been breached, he fills. And spills. We hold one another like that for a long time.

"I'm tired, Cook. So, so tired."

"Then sleep." I say it before I realize the implications of my comment.

"What do you mean?" There's fear in his eyes when he sees me get up to go to my room at the top of my stairs. He follows me. He watches while I rummage around in my top drawer, panic thinning his voice, making it break.

"Cook. No. That's not a good idea." He's read my intention.

"Why not?" I have the beta remote in my hand when I turn to him. It is black and small and harmless looking, the kind of thing that looks like it's been engineered to be lost. I toss it to the floor. He bends, almost instinctively, to pick it up.

"Leave it," I say.

His eyes are wide and uncharted.

I can hear his breathing increase.

"You want me to use it? You want me to send you into a stupor? Some bullshit suspension? Is that what you want?"

"I don't know." I place my foot over it, keeping my weight in check as I look at him.

"You're human, Lo. Humans need rest."

"I don't know."

"Don't know what? If you're human? If you're flesh and blood? What about first principals, Lo?"

"I don't know what will happen to me if you smash it."

Neither do I. My body tenses. Lo shouts, "Wait!"

"You know what?" I say turning to him, "You're right. I'm not going to do it. *You* do it." I remove my foot and kick it over to him. "It's your jailer. Or savior. Not mine."

He stoops down and slowly picks it up.

"It's really quite a brilliant device," he says, looking at it. "It's tuned to the micro-frequencies of my beta rhythm, just one cycle short of REM. It piggybacks off celestial black noise, so it has unlimited range. Did you know I designed it myself?" There is a clichéd answer to this, a moan inducing adage somewhere along the lines about how we are all the architects of our most impervious cages. But I don't risk it.

"Look," I say, heading toward the bedroom door. "I'm beat to shit. You're beat to shit. If you want you can go into my guest bedroom, lay down on the bed and push that button. Just know if you do you can trust me to push that button again in the morning and wake you up."

I walk out of the room, leaving him there stunned with the remote still in his hand. "See you in the morning," I shoot over my shoulder, as I head down the stairs.

"Cook. Wait." I turn on the stairs and look up at him. He is trembling as he holds the remote out to me. "Take it."

"No. I told you I—"

"Take it," he says quietly. The floorboards of the landing where he's standing creak with a familiar complaint. It had taken me literal days to modulate the compression rate, to coax from that specific spot on the landing that particular brittle, woody moan. It was a sound that let me believe the house had memory, history. Even if that history had been orchestrated. It let me believe that at some imagined time a family had lived here. That a parent had tucked their child into that upstairs guest room and while the child lay there safely in the gathering dark, that sound would let that child know that someone who cared about them was still caring about them. A sound that spoke about peaceful sleep and the promise of the morning.

Suddenly it's clear to me why he wants me to take the remote. Lo's eyes are dry, but his slight chest bellows with his increased breathing. I walk up to the landing and he drops the remote in my hand with open fingers. An artifact of a good summer. A skipping stone or a fractured bird.

"Open it," he says with a whisper.

The two-part case of the remote opens easily with the wedge of my fingernail.

It is empty.

"I had to know, Cook. I had to know if you would use it. If you were different."

The next morning, he is changed. I might even say happier.

And for many mornings after that, he just seemed better. The strain left his eyes and posture. He was calmer, less kinetic, more confident. He was even funny. Or his brand of funny.

He'd joined me in The Church's kitchen by then and seemed to delight in culinary "jokes." He purposely misprinted oysters, making their shells spongey and pink with an unwholesome cherry base note that he waited until the last minute to plate, in hopes I might be too flummoxed by the dinner rush to spot. The veal shanks he printed for the Rosenthal's twentieth retread of their first anniversary dinner came out chalky, either completely flavorless or reeking of human sweat. A few times, I was even out the kitchen door before I smelled something awry and backed humbly off the restaurant floor.

There'd be Lo, laughing like a skinny hyena, with his arms crossed over his thin, aproned chest.

"I don't know what happened," he'd invariably say through his tears. "Must be a faulty actuator in the memory file."

His jokes had a meaning. A playful way of weaning me off my reliance on the tissue printer. He knew the garden he'd planted would be maturing soon and he was doing everything in his power to get me to walk my talk, to get me to jettison once and for all this gastric anthropology pretense and go back to my own first principals of flavor.

There is only one thing that has dampened our days.

Lily.

She's not sick, exactly. Just slower. A little less herself. I suspect it's her time at the Water Builder's yard. That first meal of grass that, if she were a dinner guest of mine, I would have to find some way to print over and over again. Lo is right about her. She should be grazing. But I can't help a slight annoyance when I realize she was just fine before she knew that. Lo has split his time between two solo surrogacies: the garden and the goat. He won't let me help him turn the soil under our tender beds of vegetables. He says my hands are too clumsy, that I might knick a root ball. And when I watch him with our printed mid-twentieth-century tiller, I have to admit he's right. It's like watching some Buddhist monk rake his sand garden when he does it. Slow, deliberate strokes that buckle his shoulders and forearms.

He hums while he does it. Trilla's strange version of the Ambient Cola jingle. I'm a little chilled the first time I hear him tilling. I've seen what the jingle did to my Christmas hen. The garden flourishes, however. Growing at twice the rate, he assures me. Maybe it's the mulch. He won't let me help with that either. And it's nearly a state secret what's in it.

As for Lily, Lo fusses over her like a midwife at an A-list actress' home birth. He monitors her stool like a prize winemaker worries over his terroir. Crushing her little round turds in his hands, smelling deeply, probing every convolution of her colon. First, it's a micronutrient deficiency. Then she needs more phosphorous in her feed. Whatever he does she seems better. Her eyes are clear. Her snout warm and wet. Even her milk has a silky richness it never had before. But she has good days and bad days. And I can see the lure of the Water Builder's yard lurk in the lulls of our conversations about her.

Chapter 20

Lo wakes me from a dead sleep one late spring morning, so amped I think he might pee himself. It had been a bad night at The Church. Lo had finally gotten past me one of his culinary rim shots: a perfectly braised elk medallion in reduced plum sauce that had bled motor oil when Mrs. Shorenstein had cut into it. I had to not only comp the whole table their meals but agree to cater a high tea, free of charge, for about half the community of Wiloughby. It was a fare-well tea for those who were returning to Earth to celebrate the passing of the Corporate Equivalency Act in the Western Consolidated legislature. (This was bad news for blue-collar Earth as it gave whatever the sum total of any company's current stock evaluation was in numbers the same number of "votes" in regional elections.)

The only things that had gotten me to sleep that night were Lily's clean bill of health and the soothing thought that I'd only have to plate half of Wiloughby's memories for the next six months.

At least he had waited for me to open an eye before he tore off my bedsheets.

"Come on," he shouts excitedly. "It's ready. It's *up*."

"Lily still good?" It's the first question I croak.

"She's great. She was doing that head butt thing this morning where she gets up on her two back legs like a pony. Almost caught me in the face. Get up!"

He races me down the stairs, my eyes still blurred.

The chickens cluck nervously as we burst into the yard, scattering like trash before us.

"Up. Go up," Lo says. And I notice then a ladder had been placed by the side of the house, leading up to the roof. "You can only see it from up there." I skip up the rungs, balancing on the shaky-looking shingles in the thin morning sun.

"What?" I ask, rubbing my face. "What's wrong?"

"That," Lo says pointing off the edge of the roof. My gaze follows his finger and there, laid out like a crazy quilt, is the garden he had worked so hard to plant, now in full bloom. The rows are not straight and I feel a slight tinge of irritation. Then I remember it was Lo's doing. The uneven rows are intentional. I blink. And the image, the whole glorious unity of thing comes into focus.

It is me.

A half-acre portrait of me in three-quarter. Calculating for plant height and leaf refraction, for color gradation and density is my face in vegetable pixilation. It is as if he had painted my portrait with only pure intent, in complete darkness and only after months of water, soil, and sun had the deftness and clarity of his strokes been confirmed.

"Who is that old fucker?" I ask lightly.

"That's you!" he almost shouts.

"I know, I know," I laugh.

His eyes are wet, glistening widely with hunger and innocence, brimming with a need for praise. It is easy to give.

"Lo, it's incredible," I say facing him, putting my hands on his thin and downward shoulders. "Absolutely magnificent. Not so sure of your choice of subject but..."

"You really like it?"

"I do. I'm, I'm—*shit.* I'm an *idiot,* I'm so impressed." And then the darkness falls behind those eyes. He's gotten what he needed. "We should show the—" I begin.

"No," he cuts me off. "Not them. *You.* I did it for you." I take the boy's arm. I want Wiloughby to know this kid is capable of more than soliciting their distrust and fear. I want them to know my faith in him is well-placed.

"Lo, listen to me. It's beautiful what you've planted but we have to share it. That's the whole point of a garden, to feed people. To share. Do you understand?" He will not look at me.

"I don't care if they're proud of me, Cook. Not anymore." This lets me know that his burgeoning confidence was partly my doing. No matter how anti-social it is. I feel a stab of regret when I realize that for that split second, I had been no better than his owners. Could I say the same as Lo? Or am I still uselessly campaigning for the approval of a community that would never accept all of me?

"When can we harvest it?" he asks, looking down upon all the leafy and rooty and cruciferous shades of me.

"It's a miracle we got what we got, what with the frost and this sluggish Martian soil. But I'm thinking we need another couple of weeks of growth. Maybe you could talk to Trilla, get her to compose some kind of polonaise or something that will give us a few more hours of morning sun,"

"Let's pick something for tonight." He looks at me, suddenly excited. "Anything. One leaf of kale, even a skinny little carrot, a green tomato, let's plate it and serve it tonight at The Church. Anything would be better than that damn tissue printer."

"There's nothing wrong with the tissue printer, Lo," I say smirking at him.

"Yes, there is. You hate it. You hate what it's done to you."

He's right. And the bounty beneath me is working overtime to re-stoke my confidence, tempting me to actually start cooking again. But I am reticent. I hadn't cooked without a memory blueprint in decades.

"Maybe we should wait," I say. "Limits only make us more creative."

"Okay. Then under that rubric my point is proven. You said it yourself, it's a miracle we have what we have and what could be more evident of limits enhancing creativity than that garden?" How could I tell them our creativity holds no premium against their stagnant expectations?

"They won't like it. They want what they know, what they're used to."

"Then risk disappointing them. They can blame first principals if they don't like it."

It is a reckless idea, one that could seriously backfire. The rich, in my experience, are only appreciative of their own initiative.

"But nothing's ripe," I say, testing the strength of his enthusiasm, hoping it could support me too. "What do we serve?"

"The onions are ready," he says, looking down at the ring of chives that outlines my portrait. The red of the soil and the vegetable's natural green had turned the hardy shoots of the chives a dark and unusual brown.

We leave the roof and head toward the garden. I notice as we descended how my face seems to follow us. Is this a trick of sunlight on the leaves or had the boy intended this eerie effect too? I pull on the tuft of a bundle a chives. The large, firm bulb that emerges is like no yellow onion I have ever seen. The parchment of the onion is nearly translucent with a soft nacreous sheen that hints at something dark beneath. Strong smelling pearls with a hint of turmeric.

My head is so full of potential uses for the onions, I don't know where to start.

I suggest a caramelized onion tart.

Not substantial enough for a main dish, Lo counters.

A Bordeaux-infused rustic remoulade?

If the tart's not going to fly, how the hell are we going to get away with feeding them a plate of *relish*?

We could brown them then *sous vide* the slag, siphon the essence, and infuse it into clear membranes of hydrogenated protein.

"Gastro-*chemistry*?" the boy mocks. "Who are you, Cook? Some skin-jobbing Ferran Adria`? Come on! That's been *done*."

I've been caressing the bristly sun-warmed chives, smelling the sweet earthy skunk of them on my fingers as he shoots down every one of my suggestions.

"What would *you* do?" I finally ask.

"Simple. French onion soup gratin. We still have a wheel of Lily's Gruyere left."

"Really? French onion soup? With no beef bone broth to anchor it? That shit will taste like sweaty dish water unless I print about two kilos of cow femurs." Lo screws up his face in disgust. "Exactly," I say, grinning. "Look at your face. That would mean the tissue printer and you don't like that. Not to mention it will take half the day to braise the bones in that shitty sonic oven."

"We won't need the bones," he says lightly. "You haven't tasted my onions yet."

Chapter 21

Lo's onions are unusual, to say the least. They are a confounding size. Once the pearly parchment is removed, they have a sinister burgundy sheen that runs into ever deepening shades of red as the layers approach the heart of the vegetable. They have a deep gamey aroma that literally bleeds when chopped.

Baby heads, I think, as we reduce them into ribbons. We are dicing baby heads.

I don't know what he'd whispered to these seeds when he planted them but I'm a little scared to see the rest of the harvest.

As we toss the ribbons into heated butter and sugar, I can't shake the feeling that the stuff reducing in the pan was once awake. I don't share my unease as the boy keeps chopping. He's tired. A long all-nighter in Lily's pen. But he assures me she's better this morning. We are silent as the onion and sugar slag thins to the consistency of syrup. As a substitute for a protein base note, Lo makes a broth of pressure-cooked sunflower seeds and adds this to the reduction.

But I can already tell from the smell, we've missed it. We simmered it for hours. Nothing. Each hour we tasted it and each hour we were reminded of our failure, that we had missed the meaty base completely.

We flash froze it, reheated it, hoping the process would concentrate the flavors. But it simply wasn't there.

"Let's stop, man," I say to the boy, checking the clock to see if I'll still have time to print the evening's ©*Godmoth-ere*d reminiscences.

But the boy won't stop. He thinks we're close. He keeps chopping.

"Lo, call it. It's over. We missed it."

Then Lo's knife stopped.

There is only one reason a knife stops in a working kitchen.

And even though he hadn't cried out or flinched, his cut is quite deep.

I dash for the laser suture pen but before I can reach him, I see his still healthy hand clutch the forearm of his wounded one, forcing the blood to crest in his cut. I see that blank and determined look on his face as he holds his bleeding wound over the simmering soup pot for what seems like minutes.

Why don't I stop him? Because even I can smell what his denaturing blood is doing to the stock. Grounding the essence of onion. Righting the mix. It is that hail-Mary hope of the unexpected all good cooks aim for.

"That's enough, Lo."

"Just a little more." I see his lips counting silently as his blood drops into the soup.

"Stop it! We can't serve that!"

I try to shove him away but it's like he's bolted to his spot near the simmering stock pot. His grip on himself is like oak. I can't budge him so I back away and do the only logical thing any cook would do to another cook who has done something reckless and irrational and potentially delicious.

I hand him a wooden tasting spoon.

He stirs the soup slowly. It is the color of rendered roadkill, but the aroma does suggest promise.

He dips the spoon and closes his eyes before he tastes it. I watch his eyes stutter back and forth under their thin lids, his long dark eyelashes rippling slightly like the levers of some eighteenth-century computational engine. He goes deep into the flavor matrix, through the three stages of savory ignition: first, fore, and aftertaste.

He swallows.

His eyes open, dead as stones.

"Taste it," he says, handing me a spoon. I dip. Whatever revulsion I feel at the prospect of putting what's puddled on the spoon into my mouth evaporates once the flavor enraptures my tongue and steals up the flue of my sinuses.

Perfect.

But not the perfection of food. Not flavors remembered or cleverly repurposed.

Groceries are not supposed to behave this way.

Yes, there is a sweetness you might have experienced with cooked onions. But this is the sweetness of clean skin, of freshly laundered handkerchiefs, or spotless wine glasses that hold in them, even empty, that promise of that first sip of wine.

Yes, there is a meaty base note but not from an animal you can easily place. There's a warmth and immediacy to the protein funk that feels at once surprising and yet completely familiar.

A first kiss, maybe.

The taste of a first kiss.

The taste of someone else's heat and flutter commingled and augmented with your own heat and flutter until it becomes something other, something you never thought you might chew and savor and swallow.

I don't know what to say to the boy. I only know he has done what I have never brought myself to do. He has shattered Wiloughby's expectations, not with my resigned fury but with his own brand of unanticipated delight.

His eyes plead with me.

I must have to say something.

Has he gone too far?

He's waiting.

But even I know there is no turning back.

He's looking at me with eyes that are slowly softening into neediness. So, I speak while I move to the ripening shelves to get what's left of a wheel of Lily's funky Gruyere. I say the only thing I can say with the little bit of time we have left until the first of the dinner rush.

"Plate it," I say. "Plate it while I grate this for the topping."

Chapter 22

It should have been Lo's night.

I had berated the white linen of my tablecloths in my sonic clothes tumbler for hours to ensure their pristine snowiness. Swept the wide boards of my pickled floors. Scrubbed the whitewashed beadboard that lined the restaurant's walls. The room was elegant but rustic, the weak filaments of the votive "candles" on the tables casting a romantic glow as they outgassed hints of lavender and sage. It felt like opening night all over again—peaceful yet momentous. Momentous because, like that first night I opened The Church, I finally had something new to serve my customers. And they came. Quietly.

Conversation among my diners had exhausted itself years ago and all listened for the aromas of my kitchen. Like you might listen for the first thumps of summer rain after a heatwave. I watched as they sat themselves stoically at their usual tables. The gurgle of printed vintages filling their glasses the only sound in the room. I could see their alert faces as I poured, the tension filling the romantic space. Many asked to have their scented votives removed. Something was not right. The evening was not familiar. A few looked around as if some sudden noise had caught their attention. Ms. Bader-Ginsburg, the horror writer who lived in the reproduction of the Manson murder house on fake Cielo Drive, got up to leave. Only the hand of her wife stopped her.

"Hold on, babe," was all she said as the horror writer sat back down with raised and incredulous eyebrows.

"What's up, Cook?" The writer asked me with a controlled smirk. "What do you have for us tonight?"

"Wait and see," I said with a smile. My smile was not returned.

"Great," the writer scoffed. "Sounds like amateur night."

"It doesn't *smell* like amateur night," her wife chided softly.

The Church smelled that night how a good book reads, or a favorite record sounds. Lo had done that night what I wish I could have done with all my years of peppering dishes with catalogued sensory files. He would make them remember flavors they had yet to taste. But that wasn't what my guests paid for. I excused myself, swallowing in a dry throat, and headed toward the kitchen.

Lo was ready with the tray on the electric dolly. Sixteen bowls piping merrily under their caps of melted cheese

"What's it like out there?" He wanted to know.

"Like a Michelin starred Nuremburg," I quipped. "Maybe we should—"

"What? Break out the bags of Krill Krips and Ambient Cola? We either make a clean break tonight or—"

"It could mean my *job*, Lo. My job and your future."

"What future?" Lo laughed. "Do you really think it matters what happens to us? The only thing that matters is who we are *when* it happens." He watched me as I let this sink in. I could hear the tinkle of flatware when it's toyed with. They were getting impatient.

"All right. Fuck it," I said, maneuvering behind the dolly. "I'll serve. You clear."

"From the left. I know."

Then we heard the cry.

It was one of those sharp glassy cries, still shuddering and animal. A newborn. But only one set of owners had been expecting.

"Harlem. Again," Lo said quietly. My eyes were questioning, asking if he was sure.

The blankness of his eyes was my answer.

There was a Dickensian workhouse feel to my dining room as I placed just a single steaming bowl before each guest. Questioning looks, mannered offense. Then the aroma hit their sinuses and they calmed. Slightly. From the corner of the dining room, I watched as they raised their spoons. Some tested the stringiness of the cheese, pulling it under their noses with annoyed looks. Others cooled the hot broth with cautious inhalations of breath. No one spoke but I could feel them resisting. Then that resistance was overcome, slightly at first, but gaining egress as they chewed and swallowed slowly. Their faces flushed. Spoons moved automatically to their mouths. No one asked for a baguette. No one wanted a refill of their wine. I saw a tear in Mrs. Shorenstein's eye, heard her husband shush her when she tried to speak. Even the baby, if there had been a baby, was quiet. I wasn't looking at my guests. My attention was firmly rooted to the sedulous vacating of all my stoneware Provence-made crocks.

The bowls in front of each guest are now clean. Even the bits of toasted cheese that are usually left around the rim have somehow been gnawed away. There should have been accolade. Yet there was no conversation, no floated compliments, no shared or combative interpretations of flavors. It was quiet. But a frosty quiet. The kind the civilized used when a social planner has placed two incompatibles together at table and marred the delicate surface of the evening.

Back in the kitchen, I have to stop Lo from entering the dining room to clear.

"Don't go in there. I'll do it."

"But it seems like they liked it."

"Please?" Lo looks hard at me. He takes a deep breath.

"Did you see her?"

"Who?"

"Harlem II."

"No. I don't know. Your old owners are such skin-jobbing freaks I wouldn't recognize them even if I saw them."

"You'd recognize a baby."

"I wasn't looking for a baby." Lo impatiently gets behind the dolly and kicks on the servos. I block his path. "I don't think you should go out there. If she is out there and you go out there—. We got away with this. But barely. Let's not push it."

"It's already been pushed, Cook." And he is tagging behind the faint whine of the dolly, into the dining room, before I can stop him. I follow him out of the swinging kitchen door just in time to see each head in my dining room slowly turn its gaze toward the boy. It is the look water buffaloes give the lioness. Bald fear not even their stations can mask. As if on cue, the baby at the corner two-top lets out a loud giggle.

The baby and the boy who had killed her. The first version of her, anyway.

No one said it. No one had to.

Eyes finding feet, shoulders, and fingers slowing and stiffening as Lo bent to pull an empty bowl. Cups chiming loud in the silence.

A thin Asian man with a greasy pompadour and cuffed selvage jeans whispers to a girl drowning in the frills of her Goth Lolita prom dress. It is only the stony look in their eyes that lets me know they were Lo's old owners, now sleeved in the pale new skins of what looks like Chiba City hipsters. They shrink like anemones, sensitive to even the hint of Lo's touch, as he approaches.

And there in the corner, where the spirals of her cries might be less apparent were Harlem II's owners, with twin cropped heads and heavy *belle* époque beards staring at him in unconfined repulsion. As if he were a vapor of a boy.

A sneeze in an AIDS ward.

Lo seems not to notice as he pulls from the proper side, head down, eyes blank. He doesn't need to look at them to challenge them. But I'm angry. What had they expected I would do with him? Work him like a fairy-tale stepsister then shackle him to my hearth? Who sloughed him off like a faulty hard drive? Who do they think was primarily responsible for the meal they had just devoured with just-pretended indifference? I'm about to say something when Lo catches my eye. His look silences me immediately. This is his fight. His dance.

Lo has the plate of one of Harlem II's dads in his hands when the man says, "Leave it. Just leave the dishes. Cook can get them later."

The baby screams louder, pricked by the tension at the table and I make a move to head onto the floor when I see Lo reach out to touch the child. The dad recoils but Lo's fingers are already on her tiny cheek.

At that second of contact, the baby calms.

She blinks her reconstituted green eyes and smiles her copy of a smile.

Her owners share a look, at once stunned and indignant but Lo is impervious to their stare or the new silence he has created. He leans over to the man holding the baby and whispers something into his ear. The man stiffens while I see Lo's jaw work to form words I cannot hear. Lo pulls back and the man looks up into Lo's eyes.

The man's eyes are confused, searching for confirmation to what he's just heard.

Lo's eyes are stone again.

The man has tears in his.

His partner looks to Lo, then to his husband, then remembers where he is and looks to all the eyes of the other diners that are now upon him.

“Are you okay?” he asks his partner, who holds their daughter.

“Yeah. No,” he says. “We have to go. Now. *Please.*”

The slight growl their chairs make as they push them back to stand is like a roar. The whole room jolts at the sound. They have their heads down as they leave The Church. Lo has his head down as he clears their dirty dishes and glasses. The whole restaurant watches Lo as he threads the stems of the empty wine glasses through the fingers of one hand, balancing the dishes in the other.

The room is silent as the boy clears the tables.

Chapter 23

The next morning, there is a knock on my door. Lo and I have not discussed the previous evening.

Whatever we might have said to one another, either distress or glory, was preempted by Lily.

The goat has taken a turn, refusing to eat, so Lo is not in the house to hear the knock.

He's in Lily's pen, laying down next to her, hugging her with his whole body as he hums into the gamey cup of her ear.

I don't know how long goats are supposed to live, but regardless of what Carlos Yakamura and I have done to prolong her, I know it is just a matter of time before both she and her milk production will slow. Lo is not happy with this fact. He has not mentioned her grazing for quite some time, but I know he thinks about it.

He knows the Water Builder's yard is not an option. Not as long as there are Water Builders.

Goats will usually eat anything, but, even when we tried it, she refused to eat the young leaves of our new garden.

She, like the boy, is still dreaming of grass.

Whoever is at the door has come to see Lo. Has come to see me ostensibly but really wants Lo. I don't know how

I am alerted to the duplicity of the intention of the person behind the door. The knock is flavorless.

"Hello, Mr. Kant," I say when I open the door. Harlem's dad, the one who had held her the previous evening, smiles weakly as I step aside to let him into my house.

"Cook," he says. "Is it possible for me to speak to Lo?"

I am surprised at his appearance. Both physically and locationally. Not only is he the last person I expected to see on the other side of my door, but he looks happy. Radiant even. His beard is combed, his hair gleams like fur. There's not a trace of last night's conflict curbing him. He wears a faded blue Helmsley unbuttoned to the crease of his tan and muscular chest. His stripped suspenders and buckle-back jeans are perfectly faded to reflect the stress and wear of someone else's labor. He could be a nineteenth-century miner coming to renew his claim if his manner wasn't so formal. Or a twenty-first-century gastro-pub owner with his own line of craft beers and about a thousand uses for brussels sprouts.

"Lo's not here right now," I say, motioning to a seat in my front room. "He's out back with Lily. She's not feeling well."

"Nothing serious, I hope."

"No. Just age. Just getting on in years. We're working on it. Her double helix is a little trickier than ours, Carlos tells me." Mr. Kant has no experience with the vagaries of aging and his stiff smile tells me so. "Can I get you anything?"

"Some water if you don't mind."

"Sure."

While I fill a mason jar at the kitchen pump, I hear the front door open. I'm not surprised Mr. Kant has reconsidered and left.

The only citizen not on Wiloughby's payroll who's ever paid me a real visit is Carlos Yakamura.

I'm about to take a sip from the jar myself when I spot Mr. Kant back in his chair when I return to the front room.

Only now he has a white shrink-wrapped rectangle leaning against his knees. That's why I heard the front door open. Kant had left his parcel outside, making sure he had an audience.

"Thank you," he says, taking the jar of water from me. He downs it in one open-throated swallow.

"Anything I can help you with, Mr. Kant?"

"I was hoping I could leave this here with you," he says, shooting a look to the white rectangle.

"Sure."

"I was also hoping I might...that maybe you could..." His voice trails to silence as his eyes fall to the worn pattern on my carpet. He is not a man used to being at a loss for words. But it is not cognition he's struggling with. It's feeling. His eyes are glistening when they meet mine again. "The thing is, Cook, I feel I owe Lo an apology." He clears his throat loudly as he looks to his empty glass. "Do you mind if we continue this in your kitchen? I could really use another glass of water."

I fill his glass twice before he speaks again.

"I just feel, *know* rather, that my behavior toward Lo, as of late, that is I—"

"What's this?" We both startle, then look over to see Lo standing there, holding the package Mr. Kant brought.

"Lo," I say. "Mr. Kant has come to apologize." The boy looks to the man.

"Not exactly an apology," Kant says, swallowing loudly. "More a kind of renumeration." I'm confused. Hadn't he just said he'd come to apologize to Lo? But Lo wasn't in the room then. There is clearly something about the boy's presence that has Mr. Kant flustered.

"Hello, Mr. Kant," Lo says, still holding the parcel. "How's Harlem II?" There is a slight chill to Lo's composure when he speaks.

"Harlem II?" he chuckles. "Is that what you call her? That's adorable. My husband and I have been so preoccupied lately, we haven't decided yet what to name her." He clears his throat. "She's good. Great. She slept through 'till morning for the first time last night." I remember Lo's touch had quieted the child. "You must teach me your technique."

"That's good." Lo begins to unwrap the rectangle. "Mind if I open this? I assume it's for me."

"It is. Yes. Please," Kant says, clearing his throat again. "Open it." The white wrapping falls to the kitchen floor soundlessly. From the back I can see a framework of stretcher bars of what I assume to be a canvas. "There was a rather unfortunate situation with a painting Lo brought to our house before he came to you, Cook," the man says, turning to me. "I feel rather conflicted about what transpired, so I had it particle mended and re-stretched."

I'm confused.

I know I'm only being acknowledged out of politeness for I had no idea about the history of the painting then.

"Wow," Lo says, squinting at the front of the painting, which I still have not seen. "Atomically mended? That must have been expensive, Mr. Kant."

"That's not important." Kant suddenly launches into a quick coughing fit which he covers with the cologned ball of his fist. "Could I trouble you for more water, Cook?"

"Really nice work," I hear Lo say as I turn toward the sink with Kant's glass. "To anyone else, they'd never know this painting had been thoughtlessly smashed to pieces." There is an edge in Lo's voice I have never heard before. I drop the glass in front of Kant. But the man is not looking at the boy. There is a bemused expression on his face, a distant smile under his downturned eyes.

"I have to warn you though, Mr. Kant, I'm not in the habit of having my gifts returned. Not that I've been in much of a position to offer gifts, as you know. But when I give them, I like them to stay that way." There is no rudeness in Lo's voice. More remorse when he speaks. But there is no ignoring the chill that has entered the room. An exchange in social standing between Kant and the boy that I can see in the shame that has crept into the sides of the man's face. Kant suddenly clears his throat. His voice, when he speaks, is almost imperious.

"I can appreciate all of that. But we really have no use for it." This admission hits Lo like a punch in the gut. I can even see him bend slightly at the waist. His lips thin. His eyes narrow against the beginning of tears.

"But I painted this for *you*, Mr. Kant," Lo pleads, his voice cracking. "For you and Harlem's other dad." I want to go over and put my arms around the boy. But I am rooted where I stand.

"I know. And I'm sorry," Kant says coldly. "I know you went to a lot of trouble—"

Lo puts the painting down and I get my first look at it. Kant's first assessment of it is only partially accurate. It definitely has the dry brushwork of a Francis Bacon. But the summery pinks, reds, and oranges are pure Fauvist. And the treatment of the dead girl's face, the gray-green shadows that surround her lifeless eyes balanced with the congealed and wet-looking burgundies that stain the stump of her neck belie frightening skill. Its beauty is awful. Awful in the original sense of the word. That which inspires awe. True, you'd be hard pressed to want to hang it over your sectional sofa and coffee table, but I don't think Ribera or Basquiat gave much thought to interior decoration.

"What am *I* supposed to do with it, Mr. Kant?" Lo's whisper is really a scream.

"Do with it?" Kant blurts. "*Do* with it?" The words seem to hold a subtle fascination for him. A private fascination as I listen to him repeat the words over and over, each time with a different inflection.

Something is wrong.

Lo just watches.

Then the man begins to laugh.

Even when he chokes and clears his throat, his bearded lips forming a large, green-tinted bubble of his own saliva, he is still laughing.

"Jesus Christ," I say, stepping toward the man who no longer acknowledges me. "Are you okay, Mr. Kant?"

Lo just watches.

I had seen this kind of behavior before with the population rotations on Wiloughby. Disorientation, dehydration, rambling, a general drunkenness. Gravity sickness. Some people just couldn't handle the change in atmosphere even after a few days in the Martian acclimation chamber.

What did you do, Mr. Kant? I think to myself. Grabbed a little rough trade, a willing Water Builder perhaps and had yourself a little slap and tickle in the gravity dump near the holding tanks? A new infant can be a strain on any relationship, can drive one into all kinds of dark and furtive corners.

I am roused from my assessment of his condition by the sound of his hands slapping the wooden top of my kitchen table. I can see the tension in his forearms and shoulders as he tries to push himself up out of his chair.

I move to help him, but he frees one of his arms from the top of the table to violently wave me away. His other arm is now holding the full weight of his upper body, straining slightly as it does so while his other arm still waves, absently, undecided as to whether it should join his other arm in an effort to support him.

He seems convinced that the best way to free himself from his chair is by the effort of his one arm alone and as I watch his supporting arm labor under its load, I see the joint of his elbow begin to whiten with the strain.

He is still laughing.

Even when his supporting arm begins to bend sickeningly against the joint.

There is no popping of ruptured cartilage, no crack of confused bone. His arm bends backward like a piece of overdone penne, lowering him almost gracefully to the top of my table. He seems amused by his sickening dexterity. He mumbles something to himself, an inside joke he can't help but chuckle at. Lo won't look at me when I look at him. He watches only the squirming, slug-like man try to lift himself off my table.

Then Kant stands.

Or tries to stand.

He's risen with enough inertia to clear the table and I have a full view of him as he looks down at his legs. His ankles bend slowly sideways. His knees buckle backward. A bird. A great tanned and cross-trained crane preening for one last time before he collapses like boneless jelly to my kitchen floor.

I rush to him and flop him to his back.

Why do I smell a hint of springtime on his breath?

I place two fingers on his neck.

No pulse.

His skin is dry and cool.

The man is dead.

"Call Carlos," I say to Lo, my heart racing while my mind tries to make sense of what I had just seen. Lo stands silently, no expression on his face.

"Lo!" I call out.

I watch the boy's mind engage. He blinks, then looks at me.

"Open him," he says at last.

"What?"

"He's a present. Don't you open your presents?"

In a working kitchen the task and the tool that will accomplish it are synonymous. You don't think about one without selecting the other at the same time. And there was only one such tool in my kitchen that was up to the task of opening the thing on the floor, only one such implement that was sharp enough and well-versed enough at similar work that could do it.

Lo reaches into his pocket and removes his sharpened silver dollar.

"Don't be angry with me, Cook," he says, fingering the edge of his coin. "Don't be anything until you see what's inside."

I'm not anything.

I am numb.

All I feel is a remote repulsion covering an even more remote horror. Then I remember something from last night. Lo's jaw moving near Kant's ear.

"You whispered something to Kant last night," I say, shaken. "What was it?"

"Isn't it obvious? I just suggested how a privileged old cow like him might better serve the world."

He kneels near the head of Kant's body and places the edge of his coin at the divot of the dead man's throat.

At the first kiss of the blade, the wound pools a rich chlorophyl green. He runs the coin down the dead man's sternum, along the thorax, cutting smoothly and easily down to the navel.

Dark tendrils begin to snake through the long incision, and I wince at what I at first think are spider's legs probing into the light. The kitchen is infused with a sudden fresh breath of high summer. It takes me a moment to realize what is unfurling from the cut, that the sweet smell is coming from the body on my kitchen floor.

Grass.

Stiff blades of clean emerald green grass are growing out of the cut Lo has made in the man's skin.

The skin silently recedes from the opening, and I see all the man's once vital thoracic anatomy impossibly mimicked, no, *replaced* with greenly striated bundles of resilient fescue. The young blades sense the light and begin to uncurl, leaving behind their bunched endocasts of heart and liver and intestines, growing down and into themselves as well as up, creating tangles and soft briars that glisten cleanly in the sunlight that filters through my kitchen window.

The break in the skin begins to tear down the arms and legs, like a run in a fleshed-colored silk stocking until the biceps on his arms, the quads that bulked his thighs, all the major muscle groups, are similarly exposed. The tear runs up the chin until the face is split in two, all familiar countenance of what was once Mr. Kant blossoming into an anonymous patch of dewy pasture.

"It's really for Lily," I think I hear him say. "Now she can graze as peacefully and safely as she wants."

His voice seems to be coming from far away, from some corner of my mind that is not crowded by the impossibility of what I am seeing.

"Did I get the color right? Do you recognize it, Cook? You should recognize this particular lawn."

I think I see him move in my periphery, have a vague notion of him opening a cupboard and taking from it the black light I use to screen the density of the slurry tubes that fuel the tissue printer. He flicks on the black light and shines its lightless beam on the lush, vaguely human shaped patch of grass that now seems rooted to my kitchen floor.

"Do you see it, Cook?" Lo asks excitedly. "Can you read the *name?*"

The memory rushes me.

I'd wanted to have a picnic, a real picnic on the grass like I'd seen the young lovers in Fragonard's paintings do at what was left of the LA County Art Museum. Only one person could tell you where grass still grew in parched Los Angeles then.

A water cop. Like my dad.

We found one, unfenced, in front of a remodeled Tudor-style mansion in Larchmont. It wasn't my father's beat, but we didn't care. I wanted my picnic and my dad needed to look at something other than his VR porn surrounds and the accusing bruises on his stomach and back.

I'd packed his favorites: spareribs smothered in spicy sweet hoisin sauce and jackfruit pudding, a sixer of Ambient Cola for me and a few Belgian style tall boys for him.

It was a small little rug of lawn, maybe only five by seven, but to me it was a cool and fragrant magic carpet. We had been there maybe half an hour when the owner of the

Tudor mansion popped her head out of her heavy wooden door and threatened to call the real cops.

My dad had said nothing; just stood and unzipped his powder blue shorts.

He was still looking the irate homeowner in the eye when he pulled out his dick and pissed on her lawn.

Under Lo's blacklight I recognized my father's handwriting. And his name. The name he had pissed on the pissed homeowner's front lawn. I had never told Lo this story. "Cook?" the boy asks weakly. "Don't you like it? Aren't you pleased?"

"I need to see Carlos," I said.

I pushed myself to my feet and stumbled toward the door.

"Cook?" I heard the boy call as I stepped into the bleary sunshine outside my house. "*Think of Lily*!"

EVERYTHING'S IN ORDER IN THE BLACK HOLE

Chapter 24

Foxes are burrowing animals, making their nests underground much like their prey. So it was fitting Carlos Yakamura would situate himself, similarly, away from the weather and the questioning eyes of Wiloughby. He lived in what used to be the old underground service bays for the now-defunct Mars rovers. He had collected them through the years, coming upon the stalled dusty machines sent here in the last two centuries, most no bigger than mini Coopers. I imagined him out on the Martian plains with his little paws and tools, tinkering with the juiceless solar sails and access panels until he could get the small treads moving, riding the things back to his hovel like a child driving a scaled down fire engine.

I wouldn't say his burrow was comfortable. Practical but not homey. It had been built of Martian rock and concrete by the first manned crews that had originally explored Mars before their governments decided they had more pressing matters than colonizing a cold, dead and blushing ball twenty million miles away from their conflicted constituents.

I hear the music before I see him, cheap riffs played on old 1970s Stratocasters comically distorted by waa-waa peddles.

He's watching one of his vintage sex files.

It's easy to forget there's still a man canned somewhere in his canine armor. So, I wait, catching only a glimpse of him as his tiny legs and torso writhe expressively in a clear tub of specially printed amniotic fluid. I wait until he finishes, or rather, until I hear the music end, before I announce myself. He's mellow and wet looking when I see him, not a trace of embarrassment twisting his facial servos.

"Cook," he says, shaking the slick residue from his scales. "What's up?"

He doesn't seem a bit shocked when I tell him what I've just seen. More impressed if anything.

"And you saw this grass? It was *real* grass? "

"Real enough for me," I say, trying to get my bearings and wondering when his outrage will make an appearance.

"Full species differentiation," he mutters under his breath. "Atta boy." He smiles showing all his teeth.

"Carlos!" I almost scream. "I just saw Mr. Kant turn into a fucking character from *The Wizard of Oz!* Tell me Lo had nothing to do with that."

"I can tell you he most certainly *did* have something do with it."

We move into his living area, all low lighting and oriental pillows and other foxily fluffable stuff. I'm sitting on an orange Moroccan poof while he's curled into a tight feline ball.

"Carlos?"

"Lo's actions don't concern me. Actions can be informed and modified. It's the boy's *intent* that interests me. And if all you are saying is true, and I hope to Christ it is, then his intent was clearly compassionate. Compassionate for the welfare and dietary particularities of your beloved goat."

"Compassionate? I watched him *kill* a man!"

There is everything in the fox's laugh that would contradict actual mirth. It sounds like glass gears grinding on metal.

"Look where you are," the fox says, motioning to the room with his tiny articulated paw. "We're not on Earth, brother. We have no murder on Wiloughby. No one here ever really dies. They just become obsolete. Haven't you been paying attention?" My head is swimming. "You have to forget the old morality, Cookie."

"I don't understand."

"Then let me begin by telling you something I never told the pampered citizens of Wiloughby, something that I definitely never included in the real estate literature: Wiloughby is *not* for them, Cook. It never was. It has always been for the *Builds*."

He talks about the limits of nature. How natural selection is finally just a frustratingly reactive strategy, passive and, in some cases, disappointingly compliant to the myriad agencies of environment. He had needed his Builds to live among the worst in people so they could thrive in becoming their best. Trilla, Isaac, even Harlem, are and were maturing gracefully into their full potential.

"But Lo is different," he says. "So, his growth, his challenges are different, too. Listen, Cook," the fox says, squaring his gaze at me, "your mother's only sin was having the bad taste of reflecting the world back to itself exactly as it actually is. All the old prejudices and biases and genetically determined self-preservationist instincts are still fully intact back on Earth. She's just skillfully divided them into sympathetic stock pots. Each on its own regionally reactive burner, each simmering away in broths of their accepted and respected confirmation biases. No ideological polarities. No entropic threat of some socio-political eschaton. She really should be commended for reducing social Darwinism down to social Taoism. A perfectly balanced peace predicated on a base note of regionally enraptured hate. *Bliss.*"

He moved into a disturbing human posture, crossing his tiny legs and taking a thoughtful breath under the music of his joint-actuating servos. "My only beef with her is she has turned our home planet into a *crib.* Plush toys. Baby blankets. Bars and all. By convincing the world they are getting precisely what they *think they* want, she has effectively infantilized us all. Of course, this was a trend that was well into its maturity before even you and I were born. But in making that an all-pervasive *reality* she has removed from the universe its one true agency. *Chaos.*"

His dark faceted eyes glimmered with the word.

"The disrupting variance that engenders the unexpected. Isn't that what you hope for when you toil away in your kitchen? Isn't that what last night's French onion soup was all about? Which was excellent by the way."

I take a moment to take in all he has said. My surrogate role with Lo is becoming clear now. In nurturing the boy, in loving him and fearing him I have performed a simulacrum of Carlos' plan. A dry run of Earth's next evolutionary event. "Your mom fulfilled her purpose by creating a global narrative free of actual novelty or variance," he continues, as my head swarms with his words.

"And now I'm fulfilling mine by introducing actual variance *back* into the narrative."

"With Lo."

"With Lo. He is nothing less than the first being fully participant in its own evolution—a being not subject to the reactive strategies of nature but *informative* of it. The universe's first truly causal being."

"A god?"

"Oh no," Carlos wetly chuckles. "Gods are only responsible for genesis. Lo is an actual force. A dynamic *law.* A skinny little strange attractor with bad posture and teen angst."

Who Carlos hopes will reach his full and frightening potential under my roof.

"That's a lot to put on me, man," I say finally.

"You're doing him more good than you know," he says, placing his cold little paw on my knee.

"He scares the *shit* out of me, Carlos! Most days he's the sweetest, kindest, most amazing kid I've ever met. Then he pulls some cold-blooded shit like Kant and I want to run away screaming."

"He's learning. He's getting closer. Don't get caught up in the collateral fall out. A change is coming to Earth. Whether they are ready for it or not."

In my mind, I see shuttles landing on Earth, unloading a blitzkrieg dressed in pale blue overalls, peace daisies in hand, goose stepping to the hymns of their benign magnificence.

I must have grimaced for Carlos is quick in his response:

"Don't look at me like that. I'm making muses, Cook. Loving, compassionate, creative, non-reactive *muses.* Not some hackneyed retread of a robotic master race. My Builds are angels, gene-cooked *angels* that I hope, I *pray*, might one day save all our asses and make the world interesting again."

Interesting again. My God. He really is crazy like a fox.

I say nothing. I have to admit there is genuine hope in his voice. And in his black ball-bearing eyes. The geometries of hope faithfully imitated by all the servos and augmenters and photostatic modulators that make up his foxy little face.

But I'm just a cook. With the limitations of a simple cook. I work best with what nature chooses to provide. I don't know how feasible his vision actually is, no matter how terrible it sounds. I only know I had a similar hope once when I first came to Wiloughby and was so naively inspired by the possibilities of my tissue printer.

"I don't know, Carlos. Maybe," I say finally. Maybe there is a kind of inevitability, beauty even, in what he says. It's not the classic anime villain grandeur of his vision that concerns me. It's something else. Something smaller. Deceptively simpler. The fox leans forward slowly, counter-balanced by the plumage of all nine of his shiny tails.

"But?" he asks.

"But I can't help but see the whole thing as, I don't know. Too *innocent.*"

"Precisely," he says leaning back, tucking his small body into the shape of a tiny toy buddha. "It *is* innocent. I'm glad you see that. That's why it's going to take the *courage of our innocence* if it's ever going to happen."

Chapter 25

Walking home I was conflicted. So Wiloughby is just a glorified lab, a proving ground where all my snarky customers are just grist for the inner pearls of the very beings they think they own?

But what about Mr. Kant? Call it what you want but I saw Lo kill him. Was Kant really just a wisp of collateral loss we all have to choke down if the world is going to be a better place? But Carlos never said "better." He said "interesting." Historical nuclear physicists and conventional vivi-sectionists have used that word as well. And what about the "old morality" Carlos spoke of. Does foundational morality really have a shelf life? Or is it an innate part of the fabric of first principals Lo is so fond of?

I am really not cut out for this shit.

And what about the other Mr. Kant, his husband? How will he take the news? Is he going to show up at my door, mannered hat in hand, demanding answers, seeking retribution or renumeration for the loss of his partner? There are no cops on Wiloughby. No courts or jails. The whole community functions under the rubric of a well-defined hierarchy. Just like Peterson's famous lobsters. Are we all just supposed to work out the inconvenient incongruity of a Build killing a citizen by the dictates of *natural* laws?

I am *really* not cut out for this shit.

I'm muttering to myself as I walk on the gravel path that leads back to my house. The crunch of the pulverized stones under my feet is a perfect aural accompaniment to my mental jaws chewing on the grist of my thoughts. The only thing that gives me any clarity is something Carlos told me about the citizens of Wiloughby when I first got up here. Carlos Yakamura had assured me, like death, there was no *real* marriage on Wiloughby. Just mutually reciprocal associations that never celebrate the fact of their corporate expediency. So maybe, just maybe, murder isn't such a big deal up here on Wiloughby. Maybe what Lo did will be seen in the same cool light reserved for a hostile takeover. But I'm not sure about that. Try as I might, I'm just not that cynical. Or hopeful. I stop in my tracks and send Carlos a mental text.

What about the remaining Mr. Kant? Personal ramifications for Lo and me? How fucked am I?

Carlos' response fills my head immediately. I blink through his string of laughing and mock crying emojis before I get to the body of his mental text.

Relax, Cookie. If extant Mr. K is so forlorn at his loss, will reconstitute his partner free of $$.

The idea of the other Mr. Kant decorating his nursery in Tom of Finland chic is almost too much for me to bear.

Your and Lo's fates already on anticipated trajectory. Breathe, brother.

Was that supposed to make me feel better?

Fuck, I hate the modern age.

The grass that was once the first Mr. Kant is no longer on the floor of my kitchen when I get home the next day. It's not hard to find. The back door is open.

I can smell it.

I step out onto the planks of my back porch, but nothing prepares me for what I see. The pink grumpy Martian terrain that once stretched past my hen houses all the way to Lily's pen is gone. It has been replaced by a gently rolling carpet of lush green meadow.

My hens cluck and stalk around suspiciously, lifting their feet like feathered soldiers as they try to negotiate the tall blades. The door to Lily's pen is gone and above where it had hung is an arch of beautifully intricate Victorian gingerbread. Looking closer I can just make out the goat's name, filigreed in a complicated feminine script. Nubs of fence posts are emerging in a circle around the meadow, twisting their way toward the surface like corn plants maturing in timelapse.

In the far corner of the yard, I see Isaac. He is hunched over the smooth cylinder of his architectural actuator, his brow furrowed over the touchscreen as he programs for post depth and aesthetically inconsistent wood grain. When he moves the mouth of the actuator that touches the ground, I see the blocky top of another post just beginning to sprout.

No death on Wiloughby. No traditional marriage. And no waiting. Everything happens here at the speed of a basic app download.

I am so amazed I don't even notice it is raining.

I notice Trilla, hidden by the hen house. She is standing over her sounding tubes playing a moody but still achingly uplifting variation of the old standard "When Sunny Gets Blue." Is it the breezy lightness of her playing that has localized the gentle rainfall just over this small patch of meadow?

I don't know.

I don't care.

Because there's Lily, standing in the center of it all, her hard looking head and sedulous jaws lowered to the turf. Chewing slowly, chewing sideways, chewing contentedly. She looks, up, still chewing, and I see her unreadable octopus eyes regard me for an instant before she lowers her head again. I smile. Chewing is the only way you know a creature like Lily is happy.

"Hey," I call out to the two Builds. They stop their work and come to me. "Jesus, guys," I say, returning their hugs. "How did you know I always wanted my own little back forty?"

They don't get my reference to Earth's archaic farmland, but they still smile at my pleasure.

Builds don't smile like the rest of us. There's no computation, no qualification. Their smiles tear them open. Their joy leaves them as vulnerable as puppies locked in a hot car.

"I've cross-referenced almanacs from the mid-nineteenth century," Isaac begins, "creating a baseline of all seismic activity and soil erosion rates of the time so I think there might be a little settling when the fence comes up all the way. But it should be consistent with the architecture of your house." I look over at the fence. Those posts that have fully broken the surface are already sprouting little split rail branches.

I kiss the top of his head.

"Whatever you say," I chuckle.

"The grass needs one more chorus but that should give it a good moisture bed," Trilla says excitedly. If I don't hug her, she'll just keep staring at me with that loopy grin on her face.

"You two are spoiling me. Where's Lo?" I ask.

The Builds look to one another. Do they sense a confrontation is coming between me and the boy?

"He's in the garden," Trilla finally offers.

Chapter 26

The garden is leafing hard when I find Lo, head down behind the pole of a perfectly aged and rusted hoe. Home and gardening department, Sears catalogue, 1953.

"It's looking good," I say, bending down to tap the ripeness of the big Japanese squashes that made up the orbs of my eyes in this vegetive portrait of me. "Could be harvested in a few days."

Lo is tense. His head is still down, the chuck of his hoe in the deep red soil is the only sound between us.

"Lo?"

"Are you mad, Cook?" When he looks at me his face is so breakable I'm afraid to move.

"I don't know." Seeing him, I can't help but think his motives were pure. Even if his actions weren't. And I can hardly burden him with Carlos' plan for him. I swallow and collect my thoughts. It's not hard to feel genuinely good when I see all the growing things around me. "Everything is so *beautiful*. All you've done for Lily, for me. I just—" The hoe stops.

"If you're going to ask why I did it, Cook, I don't know," he says with a sad defiance. "Seeing my painting again. What he'd done to it and then just giving it back like that. *Discarding* it?" His face is a twist of confusion when he looks at me. "Thinking about Harlem. All those *feelings.* Those deep, strange feelings. Mr. Kant just triggered something in me." It's hard to know how honest he's being with me. Lo had whispered to Mr. Kant in The Church *before* he brought his painting to my house. When was he triggered? And by what? Was it the deep feelings aroused by Mr. Kant's visit with the painting? Or was it premeditated? A calculated revenge set in motion the day he was "born"? How did his mind actually work?

The first truly causal being.

Was he wired to some block universe theory? All timelines occurring at once? Past and future, cause and effect all jumbled up in his skull like hard candies in a dime store jar? Or was he full of shit? I could ©*Godmother* my conundrum, get all kinds of neural-immersive graphs and expert anecdotes about the emotional fallout caused by the re-organization of teenaged brains, the rebellious misfires, the hormonal dark ride that only ever slows into the sunlight when the crappy little car in their heads cruises into adulthood.

But most teenagers can't make soup that tastes like first kisses. Or repurpose prickly real estate moguls into grazable lawns.

I'm out of my depth.

I want to say something. And I want to say that something gently with just a tinge of hard-earned wisdom and resolve. I want to say Mr. Kant was a person. He had opinions and prejudices, most of which we might not have agreed with. But he also had a pulse and a right to that pulse and people, no matter what we think of them, are rarely best served when reduced to goat food. No matter how much we both adore that dumb goat.

But I've got nothing. Nothing that with my history won't smack more than vaguely of typical adult hypocrisy. And I've already laid something like this on him last Christmas when we first spoke about Harlem.

Are you sorry about what you did to Mr. Kant, Lo?

Are you sorry about what you did to your mom, Cook?

Stalemate.

"All I know is I've been worried about Lily for several weeks now," Lo continues. "She's been so weak. So much less than she could be. I just thought you'd be—?"

"What? *Proud*?"

"Please don't say you're not." His voice begins to break but I don't get the sense that he wants to be touched. "The feeling just came up in me, Cook," he says, clearing his throat. His voice steadies. "The potential. The logic. The *beauty*. It just sort of came up in me, welled up and overflowed. I didn't mean it. It just *happened*."

It's the most loving and confounding confession to murder I have ever heard.

Far more joyful than mine.

Chapter 27

That autumn Sunday I killed my mother there was nothing that would let you know it was fall. Not in Los Angeles. There were no leaves on the ground. No spicy hint of smoke in the air.

There was nothing left to burn.

All the California sycamores or transplanted Japanese maples, all the deciduous trees had long since dried up, their wood repurposed for export to the Christian Southern Consolidated States that didn't have the ban on using real wood.

My dad had been working hard the previous summer to soften me up for the job.

It was the summer of fun, the summer of anything a nine-year-old could want. A summer whose real conversation always looped back to him reminding me of what she had done to me that day she sealed me up in her room with that horrible piece of floating experimental hardware.

"I don't care that she hits me, Cook. I probably deserve it with all the shit I've pulled." he'd say, looking over to me in the passenger seat of his hydrogen celled '69 Nova. "But what she's done to *you,* buddy? Turning you into some fucking *lab* rat? No one deserves that. Especially a kid as bitchin' as you."

That was the summer the Los Angeles Zoo mammoth died. Either from heat prostration or from a congenital heart problem its Korean geneticists had missed. The Feed was never clear about which. I cried so hard when I heard the news that I drenched my dad's water cop polo with my tears and snot. I only stopped when he took me down to Sixth Street where you could still buy a real dairy banana split at a black-market food truck. I remember him holding my hot little forehead on the shoulder of the 101, all the silent driverless commuter cars drifting past us like Japanese lanterns, when I puked that sundae up.

That was the summer my dad really showed the strength of his conviction in getting rid of my mom. I could tell my constant blubbering was bugging the shit out of him. But he stayed cool, stayed tender, refusing me further trauma by not allowing me to attend the event of the season when the great wooly carcass was lifted out of its enclosure by an industrial hover crane. He took me to see the bones at the Neil deGrasse Tyson Memorial Science Center that was built on the ruins of the old La Brea Tar Pits. The full color replicas of the mammoths that had once frolicked in the huge pond there were now just shitty statues aging in a dry pit. All their color had flaked off years ago, like Roman marbles. All their support gantries bare as the bones we had come to see. But they still looked like mammoths to me. I remember my dad offering me the sleeve of his water cop windbreaker when my nose and eyes began to well up.

There were trips downtown to the Million Dollar Theater on Grand Street, sitting in the dark together with a worn controller in my hand playing *Ypres '17!* with a thousand other kids while Dolby trebled shells exploded off the deco chandeliers. We'd share a Toblerone the size of a baby's leg, he'd laugh and I'd wince as a virtual German five-nine threw my 3-D guts into my lap. I remember the "mustard gas" that hissed through vents in the floor smelled like butterscotch before the lights went up and the game ended.

We ate fried soy chicken and teff-flour waffles off a vendor's cart in Echo Park. A frail reboot of Roscoe's Chicken and Waffle my dad couldn't shut up about. We laughed at the veteranos who lined the dry lake there. I remember the Corp-Stig was so heavy on them they looked like oozing billboards. Most couldn't get out of their wheelchairs. Not even when they cocked their decrepit fingers into the shapes of their long lost nine millimeters and tried to school one another in the proper etiquette of the ancient art of the drive-by.

My dad had kept his pussy-hounding to a minimum.

We'd only stopped once on our way to the abandoned theme park in the slums of Anaheim. It was a titty bar in the outskirts of Commerce that still had the audacity to advertise "real girls." ©*Godmother* had pried most girls off the pole by then, showing them the light that lit up graphene chip factory floors or online community colleges where they could get "quickie" law degrees that would let them argue for the rights of women like them.

He hadn't been gone five minutes when he came back and slammed the driver's side door in disgust.

"Real girls my *ass*," he had said, twisting the key that sparked his blown 445 engine to life. "If I'd wanted to jerk off to some skin-jobbing hag twice my age I'd have stayed the fuck *home*."

I didn't see the knife until that Sunday morning.

He was campaigning for my trust, for the automatic default of my allegiance that he had cleverly whittled down to just include him.

My mother was just a ghost to me by then—not even a person. Just a specter that haunted the halls of our home with purely circumstantial phenomena. I only surmised she might have a body when I heard a door slam or a sonic toilet purr. I only suspected she might have a metabolism when, in the empty air outside her eternally closed door, I'd smell the funk of crusty dishes and dirty hair.

I remember I wasn't really hungry that Sunday morning. The smell of the frying bacon was working its smoky magic on my stomach, but I could tell something was up. Last night had been a bad one between them. Loud and hard and wet sounding. I could see the damage looking at him while he hunched over the skillet. She must have really hurt him. His back was covered in green and yellow bruises in the shape of her small fists. His left arm wasn't working right. It hadn't dawned on me then that he had a package of *Boo-Boo Be Gone* cellular compression patches upstairs in his medicine cabinet. He could have made those bruises disappear in a matter of minutes had he wanted to.

"Not hungry, buddy?" he had asked, dropping a sizzling plate in front of me.

"Where's mom?"

"I don't know. Still sleeping. Smoke some of this. It'll bring the craves on." He tossed me a Marley Gold and flicked his lighter. I could hear the impatient hiss of the infrared even though there was no flame. "Come on, man. Spark it up. I'm wasting juice." My first hit was a mouth-only puff. I coughed. "Dude, come on. Don't pussy-lip it. Toke that like you give a shit."

He stood there while I cranked back the whole thing, coughing until my eyes watered before dragging the fish-hooks of the smoke back down my lungs for more. I was primarily used to the bland euphoria of a contact high. But after that one Gold I was on my ass. I was tit-deep in the warm wet cotton that enveloped my head. I had to think to breathe and swallow but still bacon sounded like the best idea in the world. He watched me eat, his hands hidden under the table. "Where're you at, Cook?" he said. "You with me on this?" My dad's two heads kept swapping voices between them. "You up? Today we break this joint, Cook. Today is *liberation* day."

"Do we have any eggs or anything?" I slurred. "This bacon's a little salty." He shot up from his seat, hiding something in the front waistband of his shorts. He punched a button on the fridge's delivery panel and came back with a frosty tall boy beer.

"Crank this back."

"Don't we have any juice?"

"Hey, Cookie. Focus bra. Listen to me. I need you to hear me." He crouched down next to me, his whole body toned and hard and coiled like a king cobra. The muscles kept moving under his skin. I was scared. "No, no, buddy. Look at me. I'm here. I'm right here. You're just a little harshed." He popped the beer and took a swig before handing it to me. "Sip this. It will bring you down." I took a sip. The beer was cold and lovely on my throat. My vision cleared a little. But there was something hard growing in my stomach. He gently took my face in his hand and brought it to his. His eyes were wet. "I can't take this anymore, buddy. This haunted fucking house. All her bullshit. Did you see what she did to me? You see my back? I'm not breathing good, Cookie. My left arm. You see that shit? I can't lift it."

"Hey, dad," I said sadly. I felt terrible for him. Worse than I had ever felt for him before. His skin was griddle hot under my little hand. He slowly lifted his hand to my hand on his bad shoulder and held it there. "I'm not worried about me, buddy. Pop's cool. It's you, dude. *You* I'm worried about. You know what she's been calling you when you ain't around? Beta boy. My little beta boy. You believe that shit? She's got something planned. Something worse than before. She's working on some new body interface or whatever. And she's goin' to try it out on you. On my little buddy." The tears ran down his face with total abandon. The horror of what he was saying entered my head like slow-moving syrup.

"Dad—"

"I know. What are we gonna do?" His voice cracked and then he dropped his head. His muscled back shuddered with heavy sobs.

"We'll leave. We'll get out."

"And go where? *Where?* She's rich as *fuck*. She's connected up the ass. She'd find us, Cookie. She'd *find* us!" His desperation made the hard thing in my stomach start to move up into my chest. I can feel it spreading into my arms. Clawing its way into my slowed brain. Fear. Then something else as the fear cools. Hatred.

I hate her with a leaden certainty I've never felt before.

"No, man. We have to stop it," he whispers. "*Today.*"

"How?"

He reached down into his waistband and put the black carbide knife on the kitchen table. The act of placing the knife on the table brought another round of sobbing from him. I watched him choke the tears back.

"I hate to lay this on you, man. But look at me. I'm shit. I know I look hard or whatever but I'm a pussy. I'm *whipped*. I can't go up there and face her. The only thing I got going for me is *you*. And she wants to take even *that.*" He's beginning to make sense to me. I couldn't save that mammoth. But maybe I can save my dad.

"You, Cookie.

"It has to be you. You gotta go up there and do it. You make it right. You're just a kid. They can't touch you." Somehow the knife is in my hand when he said this. I don't even remember reaching for it. I stand up as he clears his nose on the kitchen floor with his good hand. "Do it quick but do it deep," he says, with a quick snort. "Over and over, chief. Like Whack-A-Mole at Balboa Island. Remember?"

The knife starts to feel good in my hand as I begin to leave the kitchen.

I'm not me anymore as I float up the stairs to her room.

I'm you.

The you that is me.

The me that is on the movie screen that is playing a movie all about what you are doing.

You see her door. You hate that door.

You smell her stale sleep scent behind that door.

You hate that scent.

You open the door. The room smells of cool and distance and camphor and slightly of mildew. The tree frogs are loud in there. Wet and rubbery. Your mother sleeps on a single white mattress on the Amazon forest floor. You wish you could be invited in here more. Her tryptamine pixel wall screens are so much better than what she lets you and dad play with. You hate that she won't let you and your dad play with them.

You trip on a snake-like tree root on your way to the bed. You fall on the cool slimy bark of a tree. You hear a flutter of unseen feathers.

Monkeys scream deep in the jungle.

You look over to your dad. Dad is here with you. Hey, Dad. He mimics the hold he wants you to have on the knife handle. What a fantastic idea, you think. That's exactly how you'll hold it.

He brings his empty hand down over and over.

Like that? You think? That's cool. That might be cool. You look to the knife. The blade has a face. The sleeping face of your mom.

You startle and almost drop it. But you don't. You keep a grip on it and sit on your mother's bed, the light rain of the jungle dampening your hair and pajamas, making them stick to your skin. It's hot in here. Hot and sticky.

Your dad barks. Are there dogs in this jungle? You look over to him. He's not there. He didn't bark. A mole barked. Do moles bark? Are there moles in the jungle? The mole crawls over the limp body of your mom. It borrows into her gently rising and lowering belly. Then it pops up. Hit it! Hit it! Whack-A-Mole. Remember? Just like the fun zone on Balboa Island. You whack that mole. Another pops up on her chest. Whack! It pops up again. Whack! Whack! Get that Mole! The mole pops up on her legs. Her neck. Her chest again. Whack! Whack Whack!

Hey mom. Look at me.

Look at me whack these moles!

Watch me, mom. Are you watching me?

Her eyes are open.

That's a funny way to sleep.

Her head's not right.

Why aren't you watching?

Blood.

Red wet on soft skin.

Mole blood everywhere. All over the pillow. Sticky like your clothes and hair.

Sticky.

Mom will be pissed. She doesn't like mess.

Dad is there. Dad likes Whack-A-Mole too. Only his club makes the red go away when he lowers it to her.

Dad, this is silly.

There's too much red.

The moles aren't even moving.

This is dumb.

She won't be impressed by this.

The moles are already red.

Whack! Whack!

One of the "benefits" of my mother's bio-interface was what she called LEF or "Lived Experience Fidelity." Your memories were recorded. It was meant to be a limbic override, a way to ensure that your motive epistemologies, that would later support your vocational diagnostics and ultimate employment status, were not tainted by the distance of time or softened by future beliefs. But to little nine-year-old me it meant that I could never forget. Whenever my memories were triggered they would be horribly free of soothing denial.

Murder that's not really murder.

Bodies rebooted for alternative purposes after their obsolescence.

I guess I was familiar with the real reason for Wiloughby all along.

Chapter 28

"Wait. Don't, Lo. Don't bend down and pick it just yet. Let's just *feel* it."

I don't say this to Lo out of experience.

I say it because I have no experience with what I'm seeing. I want to savor it. I want him to savor it too. I've only dreamed of this level of variation, even among the same species of vegetable.

I am standing in our garden.

I say it again to myself. I am standing in our garden, one I watched grow and begin to whisper and is now speaking to me because cooks can hear what their gardens say.

And now there are no more printed redundancies, no more tired retreads staring at me in the print tray like apathetic children waiting for me to direct their play. These vegetables have energy and ideas. Opinions and alliances. They talk about soup stock and salad texture, of pickling and the partners they might prefer in that pickling. Of baking and sauteing and braising and grating and mashing and steaming, sous viding and flash frying. And I want to give them all my audience, my attention. But first I have to know what they say about their rawness.

"We feel them first, Lo," I say, rubbing a warm and resilient leaf of kale. At least the shape of the leaf resembles kale. The color is a rich azure blue, a Van Gogh blue pierced by running veins of a bright orange. "You feel that? Is it naturally soft or is there some velvety cilia there? How could we help it release its best flavor? Could it handle heat or is it most expressive raw?"

I hold up a hand when Lo moves to speak. "Don't answer. Just think about it. What does it want you to do with it? Now tear a bit off and taste it."

It tears like buttery leather. Slight globules of bright orange liquid form on the ends of the veins where it has been torn. The blue of the leaf is earthy and slightly nutty. The juice from the veins is tart and unexpected with a slight hint of heat.

Cumquat with a dash of jalapeno?

I can't place it.

"Is it bad?" the boy asks. "Did I get it wrong?"

Is a dynamic physical law in the shape of teenaged boy supposed to be this insecure? No. And cultural tech gods aren't supposed to bleed either.

"You didn't get it wrong. It's wonderful. Unexpected but wilted with a little garlic butter? Incredible."

I pull a carrot next. The top is the frilly familiar green, but the root is a puzzle. It is not orange like its antecedents. It has none of the finger-like wrinkles I'm used to. These are smooth aerodynamic darts that are freed from the earth cleanly, without a trace of soil. They are a kind of clear milky color with a hint of pink, like the color of unfiltered sake. I think of radishes, certain Asian radishes and am expecting a similar pepperiness. I am surprised by the carrot's sweetness, the slight citrusy aftertaste of its dense texture.

"Wow."

"Bad?" Lo asks.

"No. Good. *Really* good. Taste that."

It is clear I will have to learn completely new flavor profiles for each varietal.

And that is how we spend the day, on our knees or crouched, moving as slowly and blindly as worms feeling, smelling, and finally, tasting our way through my entire portrait.

Lavender cucumbers that have a pleasant sea-breeze salinity mixed with their native freshness.

Black pumpkins that hide a cache of sharp, diamond-shaped seeds in their hollows. Their raw flesh tastes rich and buttery with a slight finish of smoked pork. I can only imagine what they will say when cooked.

Slowly, we make a dent in our education, suggesting preparations, ways to cut them or leave them whole. By the time the sun is even with the horizon, my old excitement has come back.

If I need any more evidence that Lo is what Carlos said he is it is evidenced in these vegetables. For a kid who had so vocally protested using my tissue printer, he had been surprisingly amenable to using it to print our garden seeds. He'd been careful when selecting the print files, reaching back to seed catalogues that predated GMO trends. Our seeds were as pure as they could be. And being atomically printed, they were sterile. So how had he done it?

It's sound.

That's how he does it. At least I think so. The way he whispered to the chicken. To our seed beds. The way he whispered to the late Mr. Kant in The Church. And sound is just what we talk about when we talk about vibrations. Wavelengths. Causal particle emitters. Music that soothes and weaponizes low frequency emissions that can make us shit ourselves. Incantations of cosmic intent. The nuclear furnaces of distant stars must *crackle.* When cells divide there must be an audible *rip.* And when a genetically augmented universal disrupter named Lo has an idea for a menu change, you listen to him.

"We can start tonight," he says excitedly.

"Have to be tomorrow. I've got all tonight's covers primed."

"Aw, come on! How about a simple salad of cilantro flowers and ribboned komatsuna spinach, then? Are you really going to say no to that? As a complimentary starter?"

"We'll see," I say, getting to my feet. I look around at the long and fragrant shadows the vegetables are casting upon one another. "There's only one thing missing."

"What's that?" Lo asks cautiously.

"Fruit trees. Can you imagine? Fresh pies and tarts and preserves? Actual *marmalade*?"

"Trees are hard, Cook." His face has grown serious. His magic with the vegetable garden is really just a parlor trick by comparison. Mars has been a desiccated rock for millennia and trees need deep roots and complicated mycelium networks where they can speak with each other. Trees are plural singularities, the one as many. Like families. And families take time.

"Come on. I'm not serious. We've got more than enough here to keep us busy for ages."

"What kind," he wants to know.

"Of fruit tree? Why not one that grows a little of everything? Pears, grapefruit, apple, and lemon. A Haas avocado or two so I can stop playing roulette with that printer every time I need a topping for my Baja tacos. You could even have it sprout a vine of pinot grapes at the base of the trunk."

"Are you serious?"

"Come on, man," I say chuckling and grabbing his shoulders. "Do I *sound* serious?"

Chapter 29

That night it was quiet at The Church. With half of Wiloughby back on Earth celebrating corporate voter rights, I felt almost guilty with how easy the evening was going. We printed, plated, served, and cleared with an automatic, almost opiated, efficiency. Our minds kept drifting back to the bounty slumbering darkly in my side yard.

No one seems to mind Lo is on the floor.

This has to be Carlos' doing, I'm thinking. Maybe Lo has had enough hard-knock social conditioning. Maybe Carlos wants to see how the boy will develop unimpeded by public bitchiness.

We'd made one small change to The Church. At Lo's suggestion, I'd removed the white tablecloths from the tables. I wasn't happy with the wood of the uncovered tabletops. The grain was too consistent to feel authentic but still the change had an impact. At least to me. The gesture seemed to open us. Expose us. Show Wiloughby, no matter how slightly, that we had nothing more to hide.

Lo comes through the kitchen doors with two clean plates in his hands. His eyes are wider than usual.

"They seem to be liking their spinach salads," I say. "Good call."

"He's here."

"Who?"

"The other Mr. Kant. He just sat at the two-top near the window with Harlem II."

"Really? He didn't make a reservation." I try to say this casually. I don't know how Carlos has squared things with the remaining Mr. Kant but I'm pretty sure Lo has nothing to fear from him. What runs through my mind is whether or not Carlos *wants* Lo to know this. What's the utility in keeping the boy paranoid?

"I'll see if he texted a memory profile for tonight," Lo says.

"Hold on," I say, stopping the boy at the tissue printer in mid-key stroke. "Let's make him choose."

"Can we do that?"

Technically, no. We can't. I remember when my agreement to cook for Wiloughby had become official, Carlos had mental texted me the contract while I was still on the shuttle up to Mars. My head had swum with a cacophony of legalese as the ideas in the text filled my thoughts. Carlos had anticipated this and highlighted the more binding parts of the contract with limbic resonance. I might not have understood exactly what I was agreeing to, but I certainly understood the import of it as my palms began to sweat and my face flushed with a cold fear.

But that was before my culinary duties included seasoning Lo's development. Back when I was just prepping and plating someone else's memories.

"If we're going to do this new menu thing you suggested, let's keep it going," I say. "Just for tonight. We can make it official later. I'm going out there. Wouldn't it be nice to actually *ask* what someone wants to eat for a change?"

"Cook, wait."

But I am out the door.

Mr. Kant looks calm. Harlem II floats in her helium filled baby carrier. Small suspensor jets keep her chunky little legs hovering just inches off the seat opposite him. There's a roughness to his appearance. A strain in his eyes he tries to cover with smiling as I approach his table.

"Mr. Kant."

"Cook, good evening. I'm sorry for just showing up like this, I know I don't have a reservation, but I assumed it would be a slow night here." He summons up a charming smile, one he has never wasted on me before. "And to further complicate my presence, I have an unusual request. I was just wondering if you might happen to have even a splash of that fabulous French onion soup you offered the other night. I wasn't really able to enjoy it the first time you served it." It's only after he stops speaking that I realize how fast my heart has been racing.

"Is that all?" I say as calmly as I can.

"Some cubed water for cutie here if you have it."

"Right away." I head back into the kitchen.

"What did he want?" Lo looks desperate.

"Just a bowl of your soup."

"That's it? He didn't mention his husband?"

"He wants some water cubes for Harlem II."

The boy folds his arms over his thin chest, his anxiety in steep ascent.

"I don't want to serve them," he says, not looking at me. "I can't look at him. I feel bad." He suddenly turns to me "He's a *single* parent, now. That's bad, right? Isn't that hard on a dad?"

And on a son, I think for a second. Why would Carlos want to solicit this level of anxiety in the kid? What would guilt teach him? Culpability? Empathy? Or is he trying to goad the kid into another emotional response that this time will render our few guests into limp coils of saltwater taffy or something.

"Was it *bad,* Cook? Was it *wrong* what I did for Lily?" The boy is sweating, spiraling into the quaking speed galleries of a badly harshed high. I know the feeling well. Just another Saturday night with my dad. Then I smell it. Stealing up from the kitchen floor. Ghosts of burnt sugar drifting over our ankles and out into the dining room.

Butterscotch.

But not just any butterscotch.

The butterscotch of the fake "mustard gas" of *Ypres '17!* my dad and a few dozen other first-shooter fanatics at the Million Dollar Theater knew signaled the end of our game in the Los Angeles of my boyhood. Is Lo even aware he is conjuring it? And how do I know that the carnival bite of what's snaking into my dining room won't have the effect of the real thing on my paying customers? I take the boys' face in my hands. Look him dead in the eye.

"Listen to me, man. Kant's not here for you. He's here for your soup. For what you *made.*"

"You don't know that."

"I *do* know that." He tries to squirm out of my grip. "Look at me. I *do* know that." His eyes might ask me how I know but his lips never articulate the question. "Take a breath." The boy takes a breath. The hard candy smell in the kitchen begins to dissipate.

"You made it, too," Lo says shyly, referring to the soup.

"An assist at best. A rebound. That soup was all *you,* Lo. Your first culinary triumph. The first of many."

Chapter 30

I had been cooking on Wiloughby for twenty-plus years, but it had taken Lo just shy of one year to convince me that all of my meticulous menus had really just been feasts for the dead.

I had been doing nothing more than reheating and plating anthems of old glory.

Tonight was the first night of the new Church.

Tonight we would still be cooking with memory, but not with a singular, personal variety. Tonight we would be cooking with a much broader, far more ancient vintage. Tonight, the memory would be a shared one, unrecognized by most, perhaps still sleeping fitfully but vitally in the dark of our collective unconsciousness, A collective that Carlos had informed me had an actual molecular structure, a branched protein deep in our brains that had guided us all toward the concept of food in our earliest awakenings.

I had tried to incorporate that idea in the group solicitation I'd ©*Godmother*ed to all of Wiloughby.

But I had no idea if they would go for it.

No matter how much Lo or I believed in what we were doing, I was still risking my entire reputation solely on the charm of our unusual produce. Either that or I was offering the kind of circumstantial anomaly Carlos wanted me to—another nudge that could inch Lo just that one bit further out of his mysterious beta.

We'd decided on three courses: a "rocca" salad of just Lo's peppery arugula tossed with Lily's aged parmesan and a sprinkling of rag weed flowers. Baked black squash with its own toasted seeds for a garnish, And a creamy carrot pudding.

We sonic scrubbed the flatware until it shined like new, rubbed cold-pressed rosemary oil into the naked table tops and filled bud vases with stems of squash blossom and arugula flowers.

And waited.

This would be my third opening night. My first one had not been on Wiloughby.

My only friend was my dad before I was sent away. But once ensconced in the spartan chic of the Calabasas Correctional Center, it wasn't hard to make friends in my new institutional surroundings. Sprinkle cayenne on a chocolate bar or salt a canned peach and I was king of the munchies.

Ostensibly one did time at Calabasas, but the joint was liberally funded under a progressive agenda and so had an educational directive. Once the warden ©*Godmother*ed my Vocational Aptitude Profile, it wasn't long before I was given access to a real kitchen and introduced to the panicked pressure it takes to summon a real meal in real time.

We were all living in a country club with time locks on the bedroom doors. But rich kids never know how good they've got it. And so, among us "inmates" the correctional center was known as The Cage.

Which is what I called my first restaurant.

The warden had given me the entire rectory building, a generous redecorating and retrofitting budget and valet access. My mother's death was positively pharaonic in its cultural impact. He didn't care if we won a Michelin star or poisoned our first patrons. A meal prepared by her murderer was publicity you couldn't buy. Which I have to admit pissed me off. I'd already had years of benign neglect. I had something to prove. I would call my way of cooking Neo-Brutalism.

Angry cooks seem to make the best cooks. I don't know why. All that furnace heat and those flashing knives seem to set the tone for most kitchens.

I had the rectory room gutted to the studs and left it like that. I made my would-be patrons sit on stacked cinderblocks at tables of crudely cast concrete. I lit the room with gasoline-scented candles. I made the center's acquisitions manager supply me with rashers of four-inch thick New York steaks and as much bizarre looking offal as he could find.

The warden didn't even flinch when he got the grocery bills.

I had the south Jacuzzi drained and turned it into a roasting pit, jamming it with smoky mesquite logs and capping it with the evilest iron grill I could find. I flame charred the steaks end up first, finishing them with torn shallots and vinegar. I served them black as napalm victims on the outside.

Cold and raw on the inside. I made brain and kidney hash with a side of Panko crusted bone chips. Lamb lung carnitas. Sous vide chicken feet with preserved lemon and uncured tobacco. I provided no cutlery. No napkins.

Patrons had to eat with their hands and daub their fingers on their home-printed Tom Ford ties.

I didn't serve a single green vegetable, not even a leaf of garnish. I told the boys who worked for me to refuse all substitutions and drop the tin plates on the tabletop so loudly I could hear them ring in the kitchen. I learned that night everybody feels guilty about something, not just those who've been caught. Everybody secretly relishes being punished.

The *LA Weekly* said my cooking was "…not to be phlegmatically enjoyed but gloriously *survived*…paying the exorbitant bill is the new badge of honor in culinary Los Angeles."

The *LA Times*: "A brave and unflinchingly honest incarnation of the country's current political confusion."

We were an instant hit.

But I was still waiting for one of those trendy solicitous bastards to choke on his jellied eel bladders (my Tuesday entree special) while I hid the Heimlich signage.

Maybe that was the problem at The Church that night of our new vegetarian menu.

I wasn't angry anymore.

I was happy. I actually believed in what Lo and I were doing. The hours rolled by. The flowers on the tables began to wilt. And not a single patron graced our door. I was thinking maybe I'd give it another twenty minutes before I closed shop and called it a loss.

Then they showed up.

Six Water Builders in their filthy pale blue jump suits.

"Lo?" I asked cautiously. "What are they doing here?"

They stood there stoically, staring at us. Through the frosted windows in their cheeks, I could see their clenched yellowed teeth. I stepped back when one slipped his hand into his pocket. He smirked and produced a worn credit chip, holding it up for me to see between his dirty fingers.

"Don't worry, Cook," he said. "I invited them. I think you better eighty-six the cheese from their salads."

They relaxed when Lo showed them to a six-top. They shot a few hard looks at me as the air began to stir between them, enlivened by their rapid gestures.

I pulled Lo aside.

"But what are they *doing* here?" I whispered harshly. "How can they *taste* anything? They don't have *tongues*."

But apparently, they had fully functioning ears.

I heard them sigh collectively as they begrudgingly reached into zippered pouches they wore around their waists. They removed what looked like lengths of soft mozzarella that tapered to dull points. They flopped these onto the table, dusting them off with no regard for the soiled fingers that fondled them. They looked heavy and gelatinous, with small tan-colored bumps that pimpled the entire top surface. Near the bases of these objects were wires of a yellowed white that ended in what looked like small snaps.

Strap-on tongues.

They all yawned, tilting their grubby jaws back as they slipped these "tongues" into their mouths and twitched their heads, like horses shirking flies, to ensure the fit. Notching fingers into the windows beneath their cheekbones, they slid these windows back and worried their fingertips in there, threading the wires down their jaws where they snapped the outputs to nubby receivers hidden by the scruff at the backs of their necks.

They looked at me expectantly, the tension on their tongue wires pulling their cheeks into false smiles.

I had no choice but to follow Lo back into the kitchen. I plated the arugula, but I was freaking out.

"Don't worry, Cook," Lo said. "There's a natural occurring oil in this variety of arugula. A little squirt of pureed carrot and it will taste just like vinaigrette."

"I'm not worried about the goddamned *salad* dressing, Lo. What about Lily?"

"Lily?" he said, genuinely surprised. "They haven't come for Lily. So far those tongues I made for them have proved an even exchange."

So that was the deal he had made, the reason he had gotten my goat back. Deep into the midnight hours, while I had tossed and turned with dreams about Lily's potential kidnapping or protein slurry levels in my shitty medical printer or a thousand other things, Lo had been quietly constructing receptor hardware so a group of over-educated boogeymen (and women) could be sitting in my empty restaurant appreciating the very vegetables Lo and I hadn't even harvested yet. How did this work? The conflicting timelines were too much for me to bear.

"So why are they white," I asked as Lo plopped greens on to six white plates. "The tongues. Why aren't they pink?"

"Pink signifies the patriarchy, a masculine appropriation of a false but traditionally feminine hue meant to signal both fiscal and autocratic triumph."

"Really?"

"No, Cook. Not really. They're white because I didn't actuate the pigment injectors during printing. Okay? Relax. They're going to love this."

Lo was right.

I don't know what else to say other than they were dream diners.

Every bite of their salads closed their eyes in ecstasy. They chewed slowly, their eyes still sealed, only opening them to gesture excitedly to one another. Without the articulation provided by their tongues, sounds emitted from them. But they were the mewling of kittens, the whine of excited puppies. Frogs croaking in gender-changing delight. I sat myself at an empty two-top and watched them with cautious excitement as they enjoyed our cooking. Something I had never done with my regular patrons. It took them over twenty minutes just to clean their small salad plates. They were exuberant, if silent in their praise. When Lo went to clear, one of them jumped to her feet, the blonde girl with the carbide knife, the naked one from my nightmare, and threw her arms around him, her hard eyes shining.

They stared at their main dishes of roasted squash for five full minutes before daring to pick up a fork. They just sat there, breathing deeply, in blissed-out tandem, like sleepy children on Christmas Eve.

The carrot pudding made them laugh.

Not derisively. Impulsively. Like being tickled.

The horror melted off them. The gamey stink of their bodies began to change. What once smelled to me like fried puke gently dissipated into notes of grassy musk and sage. I could smell winey notes of soil and worn leather coming off their unwashed heads. First principals of personhood. As happy as I was that they were enjoying their meal, I couldn't help but feel a tinge of regret. A shame that it had taken their demonstrative pleasure to let me see them as people. I wanted them to look at me. I wanted those looks to let me know they liked me. Loneliness, real *otherness*, is a chronic condition.

The meal ended, they sat there breathlessly. Not daring to move. They all made the same gesture, a quick little swoop in the air before their chests that ended in an accented punch of one hand into the open palm of the other. I watched from my seat, not more than one meter away from them as they all slowly reached behind their necks, unhooked the sensory feed wires there and coughed out their tongues. They slapped them on an open hand, or rubbed them with a dirty thumb before tucking them back into their pouches. The surly looking one from the beginning of the evening reached into his pocket. He placed his credit chip on the top of the table with a grand mocking gesture. That was the only time he looked at me. Lo, who had kept a respectful distance in the kitchen glided out to take the chip. I stopped him.

"Comp them," I said.

"What?"

"Give them the meal for free."

"I don't know, Cook. You might insult them." They were all looking at me then. Their shared glee had now downshifted into their usual aggressive idle.

Appreciation like that? I thought to myself, meeting their cold eyes.

"I'll risk it."

Chapter 31

"Of course, Cook. It's your decision but I can't guarantee you'll stay solvent." Carlos Yakamura is curled on the vintage nap of one of his oriental rugs, licking with his licorice-looking tongue the equally black pad of one of his articulated paws. "After all, no one showed but the help."

The "help." Jesus Christ. That "help," those Water Builders, I suspected, displayed more group loyalty and basic humanity than an anyone else, save the Builds, here on Wiloughby. How can Carlos be so blind? I am beginning to see chinks in his working hypothesis.

I sit on my usual poof.

"I don't care," I say, taking a sip of oolong from one of his petal-thin teacups. "I have to do this. I have to cook again. And I never could have done that without Lo." He regards me slyly.

"Synchronized beneficence? Been reading Darwin by the weak light of your precious hurricane lamps again?"

"Whatever."

I swallow the last of my tea and say what I've come to say. "I want a link to the Earthbound Feed. I want to start advertising there. Make The Church a real system destination.

The Wolfgang Puck Corp has that Bavarian streusel haus on the moon base. And there's talk of a dim sum joint opening up on Titan. You have no idea what we're pulling out of that garden he planted." Carlos Yakamura stops licking. I hear his facial servos whir as he turns to me.

"Eighteen months in stasis is a long wait for a kale salad and a bowl of pureed gourd."

"It's more than that. You have no idea what cooking like this has opened up in me. I don't dread the day anymore, Carlos. I have *purpose*, maybe for the first time."

"Purpose is a mind trap."

"Then, I don't know." I feel the acidic residue of the tea sour my tongue. "What would you call it? Incentivized selfhood?" The silver fox leans back and looks at me with dead eyes. He takes a breath he does not need to take.

"So, you're reconciled to what happened to Mr. Kant?" I try not to hesitate when I answer.

"I have to be," I say. The fox nods and smiles.

"I'm gratified to hear it," he says. "But an Earth link is out of the question."

"Why?"

"The world might very well appreciate your new culinary direction, Cook, but I can't risk the possibility of government censure of what we're doing here on Wiloughby. Not to mention my proprietary techniques of water building. Earth is not ready. Not yet."

"They're sucking down de-salinated bay water back home. Eating squid chili out of cans. Dry swallowing *krill* snacks, for chrissakes! Come on. We wash our *hands* in what's going for five hundred credits an ounce back on Earth. They're *more* than ready."

"I've done this dance before, Cook. And they banished me for it."

"Please don't tell me you're doing this out of spite."

"I'm doing this out of *prudence*. I've learned my lesson. And now Earth is going to learn hers." I stand up, almost hitting my head on his low concrete ceiling.

"So, all your bullshit about Lo being some imprimatur of the unexpected? What about that? He's imprimaturing his ass off every night at The Church."

"Cook, listen to me. We're close. Very close. I just have to know that Lo and subsequent versions of Lo are actually reaching their full potential. Do you understand?"

"Meaning you don't want Lo to continue to use people for his own 'creative' purposes anymore? You need him to stop killing people, is that it?"

"Earth still functions under the old morality, Cook."

"And that's on me? Getting him to stop?"

"Look how far you've come with the boy already. What he's doing now is a far cry from working for tips doing derivative watercolors at cocktail parties." I move to leave, then stop myself.

"Answer me this then, Carlos. What happens when half of Wiloughby comes back in a few months and learns what's been going on up here?"

"They're not coming back." I feel a chill steal up my spine. "New policy, Cook. Wiloughby's borders are closed. What happens on Wiloughby will now stay exclusively and proprietarily *on* Wiloughby."

Chapter 32

Country music is not for everyone. It's for the losers. It's for those who want to hear their heartbreak moaned back to them in simple sentences and in waltz time.

That's why I'm listening to Hank Williams yodel about distant whippoorwills on my front porch after my meeting with Carlos Yakamura.

Lo has known heartbreak. He probably even knows the avian genus of the Kentucky whippoorwill, but he has never known how to wallow in it. How to let pain and loss and disappointment thin into a river that swallows you with unsubtle sentiment before it drags you under.

I think he'll like listening to Hank.

"What are you listening to, Cook?" the boy asks, stepping barefooted on my porch. "This is intolerable."

"Sit down," I say listlessly. "Just listen." The boy stays standing.

"Is this about what Carlos said to you today? He's not giving you access to the link, is he?"

I don't want to get into it with him.

I can see no way of getting into it without making it *about* him.

Despite all of Lo's advanced and seemingly magical proficiencies, he's still a teenaged boy. And teenagers, if I remember my own varied history, never respond well to admonishment. Only love.

"Cook. Seriously. Can we please listen to something else?" I peer up at the boy.

"You know what," I say. "You're not listening to ol' Hank right."

"What?" he says, looking down at me sprawled in one of two of my hickory rockers. "My ears are functioning perfectly. At least they were."

"You don't listen to Hank with your *ears*, buddy." I get up from my perfectly rendered bio-cellulose copy of a molecularly faithful hickory wood rocker and head into the kitchen. I don't want to think about what Carlos said to me. I can't fathom being stuck here until I get the recipe right for his brand of super-Builds.

I need a little sweet oblivion. A little countrified heart-grease.

I punch in the co-ordinances for Depression-era feed corn, specifying a denaturing of the kernels in a base of cumulus purified H2O. Sour mash in rainwater. I add a touch of copper sulfate to imitate the tang of an old still and pepper in such a hint of Appalachian clay. I pump up the proof to well over a hundred and fill two jars with what squirts out of the printer's white plastic funnel.

Lo takes the jar I hand him and sniffs it.

"This is *not* water," he says looking at me.

"Most definitely not."

"You actually *drink* this?"

"You sip it. This shit's supposed to drink *you*." He sips from his jar cautiously and coughs.

"Jesus. Is there *corn* in this?" I smile and nod slowly, looking into the frosted twin moons rising on the Martian horizon.

"White Lightening, circa 1933. Momma's milk for them that miss they mommas." I watch him sit as I tongue press a fiery swallow down my throat.

One of my dad's favorite hangouts was a Western bar in the desert slums of Hemet. For a slim twenty credit cover you could listen to skin-jobbing Russians twang their way through old George Jones standards. But the real draw was the moonshine. I remember sipping from a similar jar the day I was released from the correctional center. The place had smelled of stale piss and badly cooling skin. But when that little refugee girl from Odessa got up and sang her acoustic version of "Mr. Fool" I cried so hard my dad had to drag me out of there.

"It's not bad," Lo says with a clutch in this throat.

"Sip it, now. And *listen*."

We sit back in our rockers, twenty million miles from home, miles more from the thoughts of the man in faded overalls with a breech loaded shotgun at his side who actually made the first version of what we're drinking.

Hank Williams on Mars. Beats the shit out of the Opry.

I look over to the boy. He's looking loopy, relaxed. surrendering finally to the river. He's even humming along with "I'm So Lonesome I Could Die." I don't ask how he knows it. I have a theory that deep down everybody knows that tune.

"Why didn't you ever tell anyone your mother was already dead when you stabbed her, Cook? Why didn't you tell the police or the judge? Why did you go along with it?"

The revelation comes out of nowhere.

It is offered up soft as a breeze but hits me hard as a train. Even drunk, I can't help feeling a shock that threatens my high. I put down my jar and look at the boy.

"Why do you ask me that?" My heart quickens. I'm beginning to resurface into a reality I don't want.

The moles are already red.

Whack! *Whack!*

The moles are *already* red.

"You didn't know that. Did you, Cook. That she was dead when you found her?"

"Why are you asking me that!"

"All the thousands of times you've played that memory over in your mind. In perfect recall. Over and over. You never really noticed that. Did you?"

You're not going to leave me here, Dad.

Just over night, Cookie. Just until we get this thing figured out.

But dad—

I pick up my jar, shaking. My eyes are hot and streaming. I try to drink from the jar but Lo takes it from my hand.

"I don't remember doing it," I lie to the boy.

"You don't remember *paying*," Lo says gently. "He was still going to be your dad whether you paid him or not. Whether he knew that or not."

I probably would have said something that first night in my holding cell. If there'd been anyone to tell it to. That cell of cold cinderblock, that filthy lid-less toilet, that cot as thin as a holy wafer that barely hid my own thinness from me when I laid upon it. I hadn't been in silence in a long time, hadn't tried to sleep surrounded by walls that didn't leak the violence that was happening on the other side of them.

I told myself one night. It's just one night, Cook. Dad will come get you in the morning. He promised they couldn't do anything to you. Just one night. And I ran shortbread recipes through my head like sheep until I fell asleep. I could have told the guard the next morning who pushed me down the hallway. Or the bus driver that drove the Correctional Center bus. Or the warden while I sat in his office and listened while he asked me how a boy with all my advantages could descend to the depravity of my recent actions.

But I didn't answer him because I wasn't listening anymore.

There was a picture on the warden's wall. Among all his service awards and citations, one small framed black-and-white photograph of a family in front of a plain looking two-story farmhouse.

A man.

A woman.

And a small boy.

The picture was old, nineteenth century, the exposure necessary to make it far too long to sustain actual smiles from its subjects. I didn't ask the warden the story behind the photograph. I didn't care about the real story.

I liked my own story. A story about a family. A good, regular, normal family and the houses such families lived in. A family whose mother hadn't really married the running binomials of code.

Or whose father didn't fuck and slap anything in a skirt.

Or whose little boy never poked dead things with sharp knives just so his dad might *maybe* love him.

One day, I told myself, I was going to have a house just like that. Far, far away from this warden and his office and his questions and my reasons for not telling him the truth about my actions.

The house in that photo was not totemic.

It was causal.

To have the family I wanted all I needed was the house.

Houses made homes.

I guess that thought had never really left me.

But Lo already knew that.

Chapter 33

First principals don't come easy. And they don't come free. That's why they must be practiced, diligently and without reward, if they are to have any real meaning for those freighted with them. That's why we killed our hangovers the next morning with a glass of raw eggs and hot sauce. Why I held Lo's head when he puked up my hangover remedy into the chipped basin of my farmhouse sink. Why we dragged our asses into the garden and tried to listen, to decipher what we earnestly hoped it was trying to tell us.

For three nights running, we orchestrated menus, discussed, argued, compromised flavor profiles before sitting for six hours in The Church's empty dining room before I called the night and Lo trucked what was in our unloved and uneaten pans over to the Water Builder's yard. The morning of the fourth night we didn't bother to go listen to our garden.

We were too busy listening to Lily.

I'd been sitting up in my bed, waiting to hear the front door creak shut, a sound that would signal Lo's safe return from the Water Builder's yard. I had decided I was going to go back to business as usual at The Church. Back to the printer. Back to minting those tarnished trophies of long dead days.

Farm to table was an ancient idea but clearly it was an idea not worth resurrecting. Especially on Wiloughby. Wiloughby, at least in my mind, was becoming famous for such discarded ideas.

I must have drifted off. I hadn't heard the front door, but I was roused by Lo shaking me.

"Hey, Cook. Lily's breathing weird. I think you need to come look."

Mars has no Greenwich Mean, no International Dateline. I don't know how they decided what was the first hour on Wiloughby. But by the hands that brushed the face of my grandfather clock in the hallway, it was well past midnight.

The grass in the meadow near Lily's pen was dry. Which was strange because I had expected dew at this hour. Warm and dry. Sun-warmed grass in the darkness.

It must be summer somewhere.

I can tell you now why I was thinking these useless thoughts. I was thinking them so I wouldn't have to think about what Lo had just told me.

Lily was laying down in her pen, splayed awkwardly on an old Beacon blanket Lo must have taken from the couch in the front room to give her a bed. Her barrel was distended, rising slowly but labored with each of her breaths. I'd seen this before, several years before.

The first time Lily had reached the end of her life.

Chapter 34

I'd gone to Carlos Yakamura during a night much like this one, panicked but resolved that I was not going to lose her. Carlos had come, scurrying behind me like something that would have given you a fright rustling in the dark near your ankles if you hadn't asked it to follow you.

He'd entered her pen, his usually black eyes switched to small beams of light. I watched as those tiny twin beams raced over her body, slicing her body into slivers of listless fur and a dry nose.

He'd checked her vitals. Scanned her circulatory and digestive systems. Her eyes weren't dilated. No signs of poisoning. There was nothing wrong with her.

Nothing but age.

"Goats don't live for fifteen years, Cook." Not under normal circumstances. I was lucky she'd lived so long. The variance in gravity must have kept her organs from prolapsing but hearts have a limited number of beats, he'd told me. I hadn't wanted to hear that.

"You're Carlos Yakamura," I'd said, stating the obvious when I had meant the miraculous. "You've kept hedge funders alive well past their triple-digit birthdays."

Do something.

Ruminant DNA is tricky, especially with that bovine splice you've got in her to soften the funk of her milk, he'd informed me.

"She's already cooked, Cook. And I can't cook her anymore."

Again, I didn't want to hear this.

And why the essence of a man canned in the body of a fox would hate to see a man canned in his native corporeal state drop to his knees and cry, I can't say. But Carlos hated seeing me cry then. He'd hugged the side of my weeping body with his small metal arms. I had to stifle a reflexive jolt when I'd felt his dull little claws dig into my ribs. I finally caught my breath. He'd raised a single claw to my face, the rest of his claws curling in a disturbing, human-like gesture.

"I'm going to give you a mild sedative. Okay?" I nodded. He'd poked me with his claw. My breathing slowed. My grief dulled. He'd pulled himself up onto his hind legs, the ballast of his nine tales dragging on the filth of Lily's pen as he began to walk upright. He'd paced in front of Lily's prone body. I saw Carlos when he was still a man, both arms folded over his chest, one stubby little nub pretending to be a thumb that thoughtfully stroked what was no longer his chin.

"Let me try something," he'd said. "But get ready with your goodbyes if I can't pull this off."

He came back the next day, shiny and fleet, only the drawl of his voice letting me know he'd worked all night.

Then he told me about orchids.

How certain varieties of orchids could live a hundred and fifty years. That his original experiments with longevity had been based on isolating this rare and temperamental flowering gene.

The only problem was, such a therapy, even if it took, could not be prolonged any further.

He'd talked about "gene aphasia," "non-responsive proteins" that would be the response to any further tampering. No matter how we dressed it up and goaded it and cajoled it, reproduction was nature's only directive, it's only limit. If the body senses this directive is over-compromised the systems will fail. Even if the subject gives all outward signs of health and vitality. That was supposed to be nature's stop gap, what would stop people like Carlos from ever creating real monsters.

I was game. Carlos was ready with his needle. The only thing we had to risk was hope.

I didn't know how to explain this to Lo. Not in this wonderland place that was Wiloughby. It was a woefully pragmatic ending to what had been a beautiful and enchanted fairy-tale.

"Carlos poisoned her with floral longevity," the boy whispers to himself. "He should have cloned her." He looks at me with streaming eyes and a running nose. "Now her cells are too old for seeding."

"What about an organ transplant," he asks himself aloud. "A new heart."

"She'd probably reject it. I don't know. You really think we should risk anesthetizing her and cutting her open?" I watch as he talks to himself, running through all the triage scenarios he can think of.

"Shouldn't we try?" But before he can answer himself, I answer for him.

"It's not her heart, Lo," I finally say. "It's her *time.* And she lived way, way past her time."

The boy stands and walks to the wall of Lily's pen. He kicks it so hard the boards shatter. I watch him crumble. I watch him melt. I watch his fists strike his thighs, his teeth clench so hard through his angry tears I fear he might chip a tooth.

"But why?" he asks not me, but the goat. He drops to his knees beside her and spreads his body over her, breathing deeply her still-warm musk. I watch him, tears brimming my eyes. Then he begins whispering in the goat's furry ear.

"Don't!" I shout. I pull him off the goat with a sudden burst of strength. Lo is sputtering, confused, and angry.

"But why, Cook? Why not! I can do it! I can bring her back!"

"No. You can't." I wrap my arms around him as his struggles become weaker. "Listen to me. There is no bringing back. Not if you have even a shred of understanding about first principals. Lives begin. And if that life is lucky it is loved. Like Lily was loved. Then they grow and are loved some more. And those lives give. And they take. Then they slow—"

"No!" He shouts tearing away from me.

"They slow, Lo! Lives slow and all that love they gave and took helps them die. They die. And the living let go. That is how it is. How it needs to be. Let her go. Please."

Lo's tears are dry when he raises his head to look at me. His face is hard, his dark eyes pools of icy hatred.

"You understand nothing," he says with a cutting whisper. I don't try to stop him as he quietly leaves the pen.

Chapter 35

The next morning Lo doesn't exude even a trace of anger or sorrow. With Lo's mental acuity I figured he could whip through all the stages of grief in a single evening. What I don't expect when I step into the kitchen is his air of casual efficiency. I thought maybe we'd have a quiet morning. Remembering Lily over melancholy pancakes. But the boy has been busy with something on the kitchen's main screen. He doesn't even offer me coffee.

"Sorry about yesterday, Cook. I got a little…distracted."

"Do you want to talk about it? It might help."

"No. No time. I was just hoping you could look at this and give me your thoughts."

"Thoughts on what?" I'm confused. Maybe he is still firmly in the denial phase.

Then he turns the kitchen touchscreen to me. I look down.

Written on it is a recipe for spicy Indian korma with carrot chutney. The preferred meat is goat.

"What is this?"

"What it says."

"Lo. I don't understand. What happened?"

"What you said would happen. It was Lily's time. She passed."

I can't get my mind around the abruptness of his emotional U-turn.

"And now you want to braise her in yogurt and curry? What *happened*?"

"You don't think we should waste her, do you?"

"Lo, look at me."

"I was going to make corn cakes and maple syrup." He picks up a spatula.

"Put that down."

"You want to make the batter?"

"Put the spatula down. Please."

He puts it on the counter. His face is as unreadable as arctic tundra.

"I think you're in shock. Great loss does that. After we've buried her, said a few words, you'll get closure and we can deal with this."

"I *am* dealing with this. If you want to Mexican pit roast her we can still bury her, but I think the korma, especially with the sweetness of a carrot chutney, will beautifully mitigate her gaminess."

"Stop it! No!"

"Cook. She's meat now. You think letting her rot in some hole is a better way to honor her?"

"You know what? Maybe you don't need some time to get your head around this but I do. Where is she?"

"Still in her pen. Under a cooling blanket."

"Jesus," I say, storming out.

The sunshine is unwelcome. The glowing grass is crass and as unfeeling as the boy and his corn cakes. I walk into her pen and look down at her. Her eyes are open. There is no moisture on her snout or lips.

"Hey, girl," I say. "Where'd you go?"

Her death is a slow train at whose station I've been waiting a long time.

Who am I really angry with? The boy? Myself? Or how quickly everything seems to happen here on Wiloughby?

I know now that had I been serious in my objections with Lo I would have removed her cooling blanket. I would have grabbed the aged handle of the shovel I'd printed from an 1890s Sears and Roebuck file and dug a pit and been done with it.

But I don't do that. I do what cooks do when they see useful ingredients. I dream. And I get sick at my dreaming. So now there is a little land war inside my head, small-arms fire exchanged between the practical and the sentimental.

Imagined flavor versus real loss.

Braising times versus useless goodbyes. And I don't like this emotional/artistic tug of war in my head. I don't like the timeframe, how fast the thoughts of cooking her are gaining on my mourning. But I can't think of anything else to say that she hadn't heard and ignored while she lived.

I can't think of anything less useful and stupid than standing over her ripening body and thinking what more I can say.

But I don't like it.

Like even less the gathering fact that, even in my sadness and anger, I can't wait to cook her.

I'm tucking the cooling sheet over the body when I hear Lo enter the pen behind me.

"Well?"

"I'm going to tell you this one time," I say, still distracting myself with tucking the sheet around her hooves. "I don't like this part of you. I don't mean that as a critique or an indication of any deeper distaste. I love you, Lo. But this super efficiency shit of yours is a real pain the ass."

"Noted." I'm done tucking. I was done tucking moments ago. "So, which will it be. Pit or korma?"

"I haven't decided."

"Well, you don't have much time. I'm all for dry aging but if her blood congeals any further, you'll have a hell of a time bleeding her."

I bled Lily alone, running a length of polycarbonite cable through her hocks and hoisting her up on one of the hydroponic scaffolds I used to grow my produce on. I emptied her blood into a bucket that would thicken her gravy and field dressed her as quickly as I could. I was desperate for the memories to stop, for her to cease resembling herself. But even flayed, I could not forget her warmth.

Not until I made myself.

Look at her, Cook. You couldn't look when ©*Godmother* had taken you on a virtual tour of an abattoir when you were a kid. So look at her now. She's more possibility than her passing now. Look at her. What feelings do you really have for that raw red thing hanging there?

Sentiment or seasoning?

Look at her. Look at her.

And I looked at her until my eyes were blurry and I finally knew she was empty. What I had loved and nurtured was no longer there anymore. Those raw ingredients hanging there were empty and needed to be filled. I don't know how long I stood there, staring at what finally became as meaningless to me as a Damien Hirst installation. I was only grateful there were no bluebottle flies on Wiloughby. I had Lo come out to help me carry her into the house. I was as stoic in my effort lifting her as he was.

Artists and scientists really are mercenary creatures.

Lo had already cleared the kitchen table, coated it with the mimetic marble sheeting I use when I make pie crusts or pasta.

You don't age goat meat they way you do beef to make it palatable. These animals walk around firing muscles and fat that are already full of meaty nuance and flavor. The first thing to go is her head. Lo clears it with a single drop of my cleaver. I wince only a little. The rest will be easier.

"*Tête Vinegrette*?" he asks, all business.

"Goes without saying," I answer, equally in full meat processing mode. Lo takes the head to the cooling shelf. On his way back, he notices the bucket of her offal I've already cleaned out of her.

"You know," he says, "with those intestines we could make real—"

"—blood sausage," I say, finishing his thought. It's simply ghoulish how synched we are. I watch him poke around in the bucket while I start the main butchering. "Watch those kidneys," I say, as he lifts a red fatty mass to his face to inspect it. "If you let those things touch water they'll taste like sponges."

It's thirsty work sectioning an adult animal into roasts, ribs, and shanks. I decide to cut up just one half of her, letting her other side harden in the nitrogen lock before we quit. We'll have enough of her meat for several gastric forays. I wash up while Lo puts on an old Bubber Miley recording just to get us into a real Jazz Age, prohibition mood. I print a pair of speakeasy gimlets, handing him one when he joins me on the porch. The booze will kill whatever sentimental remnant still clings to me.

The cocktail will just make Lo loopy.

"I am going to miss her, Cook. And not just her milk and butter and yogurt and keifer and cream and cheese." I sip my drink. The boy sits in his rocker and looks into the late afternoon.

"Too bad we can't milk a chicken," I chuckle to myself. Lo looks to me.

"Who says we can't?" he asks.

I'm not sure if I should answer.

Chapter 36

I wake up still in my rocker. My neck is tight, my shoulders screaming. The chemically faded quilt from my bed is spread over my thighs as if I was an invalid. I yawn, stretching cautiously, trying to coax feeling and normal movement back into my neck. The morning is bright but with a slight breeze. A breeze, fresh and full of distance. The first breeze I have felt on Wiloughby. Somewhere Trilla must be serenading the wind. I want coffee. And with that want is a disappointment. We're on milk rations now and I miss the reason why. I stand and as I do, I notice Lo's rocker.

It's funny how you can barely notice something for years but the moment it's altered even slightly, it grabs your attention. It was Lo's rocker, exactly as I remember it when Isaac first brought it to me. Only it wasn't. Lo had a strange way of curling up in the chair, a faint unease that bordered on panic. Like a cat on a raft, distrustful of currents. I imagined it was the oddness of rocking that did it to him. He had never been carried in the jostling belly of a mother and so perhaps had never burned the neural pathway that associated movement with safety or comfort.

Anyway, I noticed the arms of his chair had been slightly shiny from his grip, the edge of his seat scuffed from his feet rubbing on it. This chair had none of those testaments. This chair was new. Or should I say recent.

In a white plastic tub near the sink, I notice pieces of Lily are already marinating in a mixture of masala spices and what's left of her yogurt. Isaac and Lo are busy chopping the last bits of Lo's old rocker into what looks like kindling.

"Hey, guys. What's going on?"

To anyone else, such a question is easily misconstrued as just a greeting. But to a Build it is an invitation to a literal and lengthy explanation.

Lo tells me his objective: to infuse raw protein with a first principal smokiness redolent of traditional tandoori cooking.

Having no seasoned traditional tandoori oven, let alone the ability to combust wood in it even if we did, he has asked Isaac to help him do the next best thing. I notice what looks like an aquarium with a lid sitting on the kitchen table. It's a vacuum chamber, Isaac tells me, what he uses to get certain aging effects on smaller objects. Like the rocker. The rocker that has now been shredded and they are putting into the vacuum chamber. I need coffee. I'm thinking about Kenyan dark roast, Milanese espresso but they tell me in an odd and excited kind of stereo about the melting points of carbons. I don't catch all of it, but the gist is since the hickory of Lo's chair cannot be burned to produce smoke for flavor, the wood will instead be "melted" in the vacuum chamber by the beam of the welding laser Isaac has brought. The "melt" will produce a residue that, once smeared on the meat, will mimic an authentic smokiness that would be appreciated in east Texas if not Punjab.

It's far too much information but still I am impressed. I've printed my cappuccino before I realize I should have programmed an espresso. Old habits. I'm about to dump the coffee when Lo stops me.

"What are you doing?" he asks.

"I thought we were on milk rations."

"Crack an egg in it," he says watching the wood in the chamber begin to outgas carbon.

"No. I don't need a coffee boiled egg this morning."

"Go to the cooling shelf, get one of the eggs and crack it over your cup." He looks to Isaac. Isaac is pokerfaced.

I go to the shelf. The eggs there are larger than usual with an odd oily iridescence on their shells that moves like smoke in filtered light.

"What did you do to my chickens?"

"Crack it and see."

The boys snicker like high school freshman who have just lit a smoke bomb in a gender-neutral bathroom.

The egg is heavy. At least for an egg. The shell is thick and vitreous. It's like trying to break an old diner saucer on the rim of my cup. I have to hit the egg a few times just to get even a hairline crack into it. I know he's messing with me. Back to his old tricks. I figure why not let him have this one.

The kids can laugh, I'll take a bow and they can go back to geekville and I'll print myself a double latte and power though the printed lactose matrix and miss Lily even more.

I keep hitting the egg when I notice the boys are looking at me excitedly.

"What? What's going to come out of here?" They don't answer and I'm left to my own worst assumptions.

A square of cubed piss?

A chunk of chicken liver vacu-formed into the shape of a clown's head?

A butterfly that can quote Proust?

Milk.

The egg cracks cleanly and out comes milk. More like a stiffened half and half with a slight blue tint. It spreads into the coffee with an oil slick resistance. I grab a spoon and stir. The coffee finally lightens turning a deep purple color.

I sip. Not bad.

A little custardy, but decent. The boys are cracking up.

So that's how you milk a chicken.

At the door, Isaac gives me his condolences for Lily's passing. He hugs me and when he pulls away there are tears in his eyes. Seeing his tears chases out of my eyes the rogue sadness I'm still feeling when I think about Lily. I want to ask him how Lo has gotten over her death so quickly, so efficiently. I'd had years to let her go but Isaac seems more torn up over losing her than Lo. But I don't say anything.

Lo is Lo.

Chapter 37

The split-rail fence that surrounds Lily's yard has grown in nicely. But what will it hold? The sign above her pen is carved beautifully. But who will it name? It's a lovely scene. Pastoral. Peaceful. Perfectly congruent with the pretend provenance of my house. But useless. A testament to research and execution with no utility. Much like the goat meat waiting to be smoked in my kitchen. Who will eat it? Probably not the remaining citizens of Wiloughby. And definitely not the Water Builders. Cooking her is academic. An exercise in the possible, which is exactly what Wiloughby, now free of its pretense of being a community, is revealing itself to be.

I am so congested with these thoughts I almost don't notice it. It's shrouded under some wilted Romain and a few strawberry tops. I've come to the compost heap to dump the eggshells.

Vegetable waste doesn't smell like this.

Death stink.

I pick off the rotted lettuce and almost leap back in shock.

One of my chickens.

Its feathers are matted and moist, its tiny eyes not quite closed under their creased black eyelids. I poke the head. It lolls to one side. Its neck has been broken.

But that's not what is surprising.

What's surprising is this chicken has udders.

Just under the breast the feathers thin to a bloated pimpled sack that extends clear back to its tail feathers. On the sack are four puckered skin tags with tiny holes at their tips. I push the sack and a thick amber colored ooze steals through the holes. It smells strongly of sulfur.

It's been less than twenty-fours hours since I was clearly mistaken when I thought I'd been joking about milking a chicken. Less than twenty-four hours and I've tasted his response to my not-gotten joke in my morning coffee.

I'm beta boy all over again.

Just another lackey assisting yet another emotionally constipated genius realize their potential.

But why is the neck broken? Had he used the blue ribbon again to put the creature out of its freakish misery? Had the unholy union of two distinct denizens of the farmyard proven ultimately irreconcilable and the thing had died of "natural" causes?

Or had Lo just seen the result, scoffed at the inelegance of it and snapped its neck without a thought?

"Cook?"

I almost jump out of my skin at the sound of my name.

"Jesus, Carlos. You scared the shit out of me."

"What have you got there?" I step aside to give Carlos a clear view of the dead bird. I can only imagine how the thing must appear to a creature of Carlos' scale. If he's disturbed by what he sees he doesn't show it.

"Interesting," he says, after he's sniffed it in a quick canine fashion. "He got the gross morphology right but clearly not the function."

"Oh, he got it right. I cracked an egg filled with heavy cream into my coffee this morning." Carlos rummages in the compost pile and comes up with the eggshells I had just tossed there.

"Vitreous calcium. Clearly printed."

"So a *hen* didn't lay that?" As if that small blessing might offer some relief. "I don't get it. It was just a joke. We were drunk and I—"

"You got him *drunk*?" I feel a stab of panic.

"Yeah. Lily had just died. Did I—?"

"No. It's just a variable in his development I never thought of."

"Should we be worried?"

"Possibly," the fox says, snaking past my ankles. "Follow me." He scampers ahead as I begin to walk. He waits for me to catch up. "Compared to what I'm about to show you," he says, slowing his pace, "that thing in the compost heap is just an *amuse bouche*."

Chapter 38

I recognize the house from having passed it several times, but I only know whose residence it is from Lo's description of it.

A white frozen orchid big enough to live in.

The home of Mr. and Mr. Kant.

Carlos needs a boost to reach the front door scanner. He peers into the scanner and it ignites to life. "Yakamura, Carlos, security voice print override," he purrs. "*With courage, all things are possible.*" The seals around the front door dissolve into the jamb and Carlos motions for me to push the door open. A cloud of frosted air billows past my face as Carlos drops soundlessly from my arms and skitters into the house.

It's freezing inside, so cold my breath fogs. The walls are blank in the foyer. The massive screens blank and milky in the dim light. I follow him into the expansive living room. Everything is covered with a glittering sheen of permafrost. The furniture is as blank as the walls, just soft modular shapes vaguely suggestive of sitting and drinking and conversation, waiting apparently to glow with specificity at the owner's request. But no one's here.

At least I don't think there is.

I am about to follow Carlos deeper into the house when my heart jumps. Something darts across the wall from the corner of my eye.

Standing right in front of me is a short-bearded man in a furry parka and leggings holding a flint-tipped spear. His features are dark and prognathic, softly ape-like. I reach out to touch the man. He is not flesh. His surface is hard but hollow. A plaster cast projected by the home's tryptamine actuators. I recognize him immediately.

Why this? Why here?

"That look familiar to you?" Carlos asks. I nod, my body tense and jaw slack. "Good. Maybe what's in the bedroom will make sense to *you,* then."

The walls are ice in the bedroom, hard convolutions of wind-shaped gouges and edges, deep blue at the roots. They are freezing cold when I touch them. I notice a soft snow is falling in the room. Gathering like down on the small outcroppings that jut out from the walls, piling up on the floor. Completely obscuring the thing laid out on the bed.

"What is that, Carlos?"

"Again, I was hoping you might tell me."

I step to the bed. I bend over what looks obscurely like a human body with an odd arch over its chest covered in light snow.

I see two white low mounds that could be legs.

They end into two higher mounds that could be feet.

I have no idea what the arch is.

The rest of it, what might be a torso, arms, and head is just an unrecognizable mass. I blow away the snow where the head should be. The delicate crystals drift away revealing what looks like hair. Long, tangled blonde and darker blonde strands matted into hanks that seem to cover every inch of the thing.

Only it's not hair.

It's too thick and musky-smelling to be hair.

Its fur. Ancient fur.

I use my hands to clear the rest of the snow from the head. Just to confirm my suspicions.

The face, or what should have been the face, is too buried in fur to be recognizable. I can see two small brown eyes sunk deep into the shaggy brow, frozen tears darkening the fur of the lower lids. The eyes have been pushed almost to the sides of the face to accommodate the bulby mass that broadens the bridge of what was once a nose before it snaked past the thing's chest.

A trunk. The thing has a trunk.

The top lip reveals a grayish pink as it curls away, is forced away really, from what look like two massive yellowed shafts that grow out of the top jaw. I follow the trajectory of these shafts, as they break the air perpendicular to the chest before their weight had forced the chin to the top if the sternum, looping elegantly backward before tapering into two crudely cut cylinders. The arch over the chest is the thing's tusks. Tusks with their tips cut off.

This poor thing on the bed should summon nothing but nightmares. But it's not horror I feel when I look at it. And

I also have a suspicion it was not horror that inspired the boy who made it.

"At least its blood is unaltered," Carlos says from somewhere near my knees. "I ran a quick DNA diagnostic the first time I was here. I was wondering why I never received a wrongful death complaint from Harlem's remaining owner."

Where is the baby? Where is Harlem II?

"It's the mammoth from the LA Zoo my dad took me to see when I was kid." Carlos just stares at me. "The one that died," I continue, "and—"

"What, Cook?"

"Made me sadder than I've ever been before."

"Did Lo know about this memory of yours?"

"Would that matter? It didn't matter with the grass." Carlos begins to circle the room in a slow sleek walk, all nine of his tails bobbing gently behind him.

"How was Lo the day Lily died?"

"Inconsolable. Totally crushed."

"And the next day?"

"He was fine. More than fine." Carlos stops pacing and jumps up on the bed to face me.

"This is why, Cook. This thing on the bed is *why*. Don't you get it? This thing was not inspired by his loss and sorrow, by his fear of a possible recrimination from Kant. It *is* his loss and sorrow. And fear. Compartmentalized. *Manifest.*"

"But he surely has enough shitty memories of his own?"

The endless humiliation of parading his selected skills before his owner's party guests. Those nights of forced stupors alone on his Shelf when he was of no use to anyone.

"Why is he using *my* memories, Carlos?"

"He's not. Technically, he's using the way you *remember* your memories." The look of confusion on my face is enough to make the fox assume a more professorial stance. "My major hope with the Builds was that I could encourage in them positive incentives in their acquired experiences. In my studies, the one thing every cognitive researcher and ascended spiritual master agree upon is that we must make constant assertive effort to avoid negative thoughts. Feelings of worthlessness, shame, guilt. Those are the real barriers to individual success. And those bad feelings and thoughts in us are inevitably triggered, not by what we remember about our experiences. But *how* we remember. The Builds remember what happens to them. You can't tinker with a million-plus years of inherited cognitive evolution. But you can modify it. Genetically. You can select for a predisposition toward the positive. Regardless of cultural programming. That's what Wiloughby has proven."

"But Lo is different."

"Precisely. His developmental pressures are different from the other Builds."

"You mean me?"

"The pain of your past is enormous, Cook. That's why I chose you. By loving him and him loving you, you've become mutually formative in your individual expressions of self-hood. The good. And the bad."

There was only one thing wrong with what Carlos was telling me. Choice. His theory never mentioned choice. How the effect of one's choices are manifest in their repercussions. Carlos sees Wiloughby as a glorified research facility. To me, it's my home. He sees Lo as a compendium of manipulated genetic expressions. Nothing more. Three people dead seemed a fair price to pay for confirmation of the boy's intended development. But to me Lo is a person. A boy. *My* boy. And he has the right to understand what it costs to be a person.

That's why I think he needs to know.

Lo needs to see the mammoth he had made out of his sorrow. He needs to touch it to know it no longer moved. To know that he had made something this time that did not nourish something he loved or improve the artistic utility of someone he once loved. He needs to know that what he had done had no benefit at all for another creature. Other than that part of himself he did not know he had become.

Chapter 39

I could smell the smoky perfume of Lo's tandoori korma feast before I could even see The Church. If he'd sent a group solicitation to all of Wiloughby letting them know meat was back on the menu he needn't have bothered. They were already lined up outside the restaurant when I strode up. Everyone but the Water Builders.

"My, God, Cook. That smells divine," Mrs. Shorenstein quips as I pass.

"You've really outdone yourself this time," the horror writer's partner smirks. On and on, fawning over me like I was returning K-pop star. What I would have given to hear such accolades even a week ago. And there I was, sauntering into my heavenly smelling kitchen about to tear the boy from his magic night.

"It smells great."

"Where have you been?" the boy says nervously. "I hope we have enough. Can you heat up the aloo gobi?"

"Lo, you have to come with me."

"What? When?"

"Now. Right now."

"Did you see the line? We're at full capacity tonight."

"That's marvelous. But I don't care. We need to go."

"No," he says, with a chilling finality. "*Not* right now. It can wait until closing."

"Lo, listen to me. I have a shitload of chafing dishes, we can set the meal up buffet style."

"But I want to see their *faces*."

"You've already *seen* their faces. There's something else you need to see." I grab his arm. He pulls away.

"I said no, Cook!" The fury on his face is terrifying. I breathe deeply to try to stay calm but I'm scared.

"What are you going to do, Lo?" I say, hoping my voice doesn't break and betray the calm I'm trying so hard to fake. "You going to turn *my* knees to grass and buckle *me* to the ground? You going to grow udders on *my* belly and crack *my* neck? (*turn me into some wooly mammoth minotaur?*) What?" I watch his face soften.

"Tonight's special, Cook. Why are you doing this?"

"I could ask you the same question. Come with me, please."

And maybe both of us will get answers.

I feel him petulant and sullen behind me but still he follows. He looks confused when he sees the house where I stop, the huge orchideous roof glowing eerily in the early evening light. He enters the house cautiously while I hold open the door.

It is still unlocked.

Had Carlos known of and accommodated my instructional plan?

He moves slowly though the cold ghostly rooms. When he sees the cave man, he stops, his mind producing its own conclusions, stoking its own dread.

"Cook," he whispers. "I didn't know."

"That's the problem. Come on."

It's stopped snowing in the bedroom. Maybe the boy's ascending anxiety has shunted the tryptamine actuators. The flurries have melted giving the boy a clean and unobstructed view of the thing on the bed.

What would it be like to look your anger in eyes that were not your own? To be able to touch the cold dead mass of your own sorrow?

I know this cannot be easy. But I see no other way. He's stopped by the bedroom door. His head is down so I cannot read his face. I take his hand.

"Come on," I say softly. "You don't have to do this alone. I'm right here."

I ask him if he recognizes what is on the bed. His look tells me he does. I tell him to go closer. To touch it. To smell it. Does he know *who* that once was? His look tells me he does not. I don't expect this. I thought at least he would know the thing's identity. But I don't labor the point. I agree with Carlos that actions can be modified. But only after intent is clarified.

He'd had no intent this time.

So how can it be clarified?

I have to keep it simple so he can understand why I brought him here. So *I* can understand why I brought him here. That's why I have to go slow. Carlos might call it the old morality, but I still think it's wrongful death. Even though Carlos has told me there is no real death on Wiloughby. Just wrongful then.

I'm standing right next to him so I can feel him tremble. Or maybe it's me that's trembling.

Like I said, it's all very confusing in a world with very few absolutes like Wiloughby.

"That's Mr. Kant's husband," I say. The boy says nothing. "Actions have consequences, Lo. And in your case, feelings *are* actions. People are getting…" (I chose my word with what I hope is technical precision) "…*hurt.* Worse than hurt. Do you understand?" How do you tell a child that just because they have the ability to do something does not justify them doing it? So-called adults from Oppenheimer to Werner Von Braun didn't understand this. The kid doesn't need a lecture. He needs love. He needs me to take the long way around. "When I took the rap for my dad, a pretty good part of myself knew what I was doing. Knew why I was doing it. I didn't want to admit this to myself. But I still knew it. He might have been the worst dad in the world in many ways, but he was still my dad. You were right when you reminded me of this. And I did it because I loved him. Even if I never wanted to see him again. Keeping him out of jail put me in one. Even after I was released. My life never got better. Not until I met you."

He steps back from the bed and looks at me.

"I don't know how stop."

"Yes, you do. Even for people like me feelings should only inform your reality. Never shape it. And you're more like me than you know."

What does it profit a man if he gains the whole world but loses his soul? Corny and oddly apropos.

"You don't know what it's like. They're too strong. Especially for Lily."

"You're stronger." He won't look at me.

"Look at that thing on the bed, Lo. You *have* to be stronger."

"I'm a mistake, Cook," he says coldly. "Carlos made a mistake with me."

"I can cook, Lo," I begin haltingly, "but not even *close* to the way you can cook. I can plant a garden but nowhere *near* the caliber of the magnificent menagerie you created. I could even love Lily. But I couldn't show her my love the way *you* did. I'm myself again because of you. Do you know that? Every living thing has a right to live. And if we take that life for our own sustenance then we have to own that. Honor that in the way we choose to continue living. Harlem's death I understand. Kind of. The first Mr. Kant you did for Lily. Okay. But this Mr. Kant? What is it in what you have done to him that could possibly sustain you?"

ANTICIPATION DAY

Chapter 40

On Wiloughby the "birth" of a Build is not an event or yet a blessing so there is no reason to remember that day. Much less celebrate it. Instead, their owners wait for that first anticipatory tingle when their "child" maybe draws something with even a hint of compositional nuance, or stacks blocks in a way that might pass for Post-Modern Revisionism instead of pre-cognitive toddlerism.

They call that day Anticipation Day.

There are no cake or candles, no gifts, no tail-less donkeys braying from liquid pixel screens guiding blind pins into their 3-D posteriors.

The kids just get a double ration of whatever goop they are fed to keep their synapses firing and the owners get to enforce a desired behavior while they wait for their "investments" to mature.

I've had to ask Trilla the date of Lo's Anticipation Day, made her swear to secrecy once I've told her my plan. Builds share a connection I don't fully understand so keeping a secret between them is probably more arduous for her than I realize. But she graciously agrees.

I've decided to build Lo his own room, a separate building still connected to the main house, in the footprint of Lily's old pen. Isaac tells me this might take some time. Not for the new room to sprout but for Lily's old one to decompose.

Nothing is wasted on Wiloughby, not even the cellulose atoms Isaac uses in his construction. To demolish the old shed, Isaac has had to inject it with a "quark virus," a kind of atomic de-bonding sickness that eats away at the old structure and is reabsorbed into the soil.

I've planned a little party, just me and the Builds and a simple white cake smothered in dark chocolate ganache with sixteen LED "candles" that Isaac has rigged to flicker then shunt with a blow of Lo's breath. To keep it a surprise I have sent Lo to the garden to hoe out all the dead growth and mulch the new furrows before he re-seeds them. The task that should take him the best part of a day.

Lily's pen looks like a ruin in a painting from the Romantic Era as it dissolves upon the green of her meadow. It is hard to see the elegant glyphs that once formed her name above her enclosure rot away to crystals that fall like ash to the grass. But the new structure will be beautiful. At least I hope Lo will think so. He's a hard boy to read and we really haven't discussed his architectural preferences.

So I'm taking a chance. I could feel his pain when he told me about his first meeting with Harlem's owners the day his painting was rejected, but I could swear I detected just a touch of admiration when he described their house. He is a creature designed for future generations after all, so I'm pretty confident he will appreciate a building both organic and modern.

Isaac is excited because it will give him a chance to realize his new architectural direction. "Living" dwellings, Isaac has called them. A building made of "variable density" atoms that can change the speed of their structural vibrations and so change at their owner's whim. A 2.0 version of Wiloughby's old tryptamine screens. For the purposes of presentation, he has decided on a circular floor plan that spirals up into a second story. His model looks like an albino escargot shell, both elegant and ruminative. A perfect place for Lo to find the rest of himself.

Trilla has composed a clear day, a Joshua Tree desert morning spiced with the smell of sage brush and the promise of afternoon heat. I've just poured the dark shell of my ganache over the cake and step out to the meadow to see how the building is coming. Everything is going according to plan.

Everything but the sound of my name whispered by a ghost.

"Hey, Cook. I hope I'm not intruding." It's the second Mr. Kant.

He's not some frosty mammoth decomposing on his bed. He's a very much living man. The shock is so severe I can't swallow.

"I'm sorry if I shocked you. I know it's been a while."

Two years to be exact. Two earth equivalent solar cycles of a relatively normal life with Lo and the rest of Wiloughby. Cooking eggs Florentine for Sunday brunch and real chicken dinners on Sunday night at The Church. Lo's been as sullen and secretive as any regular teenager during these years. Perfecting his beurre blanc. Cultivating a variety of broccoli rabe that tastes faintly like smoked salmon.

"I don't know what to say? I thought you were—?"

"What was it Mark Twain once said about the rumors of one's death?" He looks thin and tired. I notice he has changed his hair. It's no longer an imitation of the close utilitarian crop of his husband's hair.

His dead husband's hair.

It's now styled in a neat high pompadour colored a songbird orange that fades to canary yellow at his long sideburns. I'd say he'd dyed it. But I know better. Wherever he's been, however he's managed to handle the stress of his disappearance, he's still found time to get a full hair follicle transplant. I just stare at him, dumbfounded. I'm so surprised I don't notice what's dangling playfully at his side.

Harlem II.

"I wouldn't say no to a cup of tea," he says. "If it's no trouble."

I brew a pot of Earl Grey to hide the bitterness of the valerian drops I've put in the pot to hopefully soothe him. His hands are shaking, even clasped together on the top of my kitchen table.

"Thank you," he says, when I bring the tea to the table. "This is lovely."

I don't know what to say.

The air between us is charged with questions both unanswered and unasked.

I wait for him.

He sips, his cup unsteady at his lips.

"I'm sorry if this seems like an imposition but I really had no choice but to come here." He sips again after I say nothing. "She's not really much like her former self, this new version of Harlem. She's...well, *advanced.* And I thought what with you and Lo, you might be able to provide some insight." So that's why he's come? To get some friendly Build-raising advice? Where the hell has he been? Who was that moldering two years ago on his mega thread count Egyptian cotton sheets? I will have to wait for answers.

"How can I help, Mr. Kant?"

I glance over at Harlem II while he sips his tea. She's a redhead like her predecessor. Coffee-colored freckles dapple her plump pale skin and cheeks. But the green of her eyes is not a fresh summer green. They are a troubled green. A deep mossy pond green with a circle of bright amber around the pupil.

"She's lovely. Really quite lovely." The child looks at me while her owner speaks. She knows she is being discussed, "But sometimes when I'm playing with her or giving her a bath or whatever one is supposed to do, the way she looks at me, how her little face can suddenly grow so serious, I'd swear she knows what I'm thinking. That she can read my thoughts and what's more, actually understand them. Does that sound odd?"

Had Carlos sold him an upgrade of Lo's generation?

"Not at all," I say. "There's nothing wrong with you, honey. Is there." Harlem II just looks back at me, a cynical smile on her face. Obviously, she knows when she's being patronized.

"Oh, she doesn't speak. She doesn't even cry. She just stares at you like that."

"Just the other day I'd given her some of that polymer clay to play with, you know the kind that hardens once it's no longer softened by body heat. I think I'd read somewhere on the Feed how manual dexterity, especially in children selected for future physical expression, are well-served by giving them such substances. I didn't think much about it until I saw she had made this."

He places a bright pink waxy figure on the table. It's really no more crude than Picasso's experiments with sculpture, more representational if anything. Anyone could see what it is supposed to be. A small pink man with the head of a mammoth.

"She told me to give this to Lo. That he would understand." I don't ask how she has told her owner what to do. I think I know. I pick it up. The tusks bend gently to the chest. Her tiny fingernails have even raked the face and body to simulate thick fur.

"Jesus," I whisper. The man's face is a mask of youthful fear, not diminished in the slightest by his sherbet-colored hair. "Were you there, Mr. Kant? When it happened?"

"Was I there?" he smiles sickly. "I *saw* it, Cook. I saw it *happen* to him."

The second Mr. Kant wasn't like the rest of Wiloughby. He hadn't come from money or the spiritual disuse that comes from a childhood of ease. He was a dancer. The owner of his own internationally recognized modern troupe. But when the National Endowment for the Arts had dried up and gone regional, he'd defaulted to a different type of dancing. Through the bars of his go-go cage situated above the cruising floor of a fisting club in Silverlake he had watched the funds that had once kept his dance company afloat sluice through the crooked culverts of local bureaucracies.

"Rufus knew who I was when he met me. Rufus was my late husband's name. He probably never introduced himself to you." I just shake my head and don't ask the name of my guest. "Everyone who worked that club knew Rufus Kant was a catch. Especially me, broke as I was. But I was very transparent about my I predilections. We even shared them. At first. But Rufus Kant was a traditionalist at his core. When I had my first bout with Corp-Stig, really a quite elegant welt that spelled *Laboutin* with a darling little high-heeled mule beneath it, he'd paid for my round of vaccinations. Not cheap."

I remember my father wasn't so thrilled when the words "Marley Gold" first rose angry and oozing on his ass. I never asked what it had cost my mother to have it erased.

"He wanted to make an honest man of me. And that wasn't really conceivable on Earth, not with all those inviting temptations trolling Sunset Junction in charming home-printed couture. So I married him. In the captain's quarters on the Israeli Space Station. Convenient, really. He'd just brokered the deal for the remaining hectares of Gaza and he needed the Prime Minister's retinal scan to close the deal. Two birds, you see. Does it really matter if you take your vows in Hebrew, stepping on a perfectly decent vase of Baccarat crystal even if you were born Baptist? The Lord loves us all. Wiloughby was supposed to be a new beginning for us. A clean slate. There was nothing in the solicitation literature about how delectable the Water Builders might prove to be."

"So that thing on your bed—?"

"We never exchange names. That's part of the allure." He sips his tea. The valerian has begun to work its magic. "But the Water Builders *are* dangerous, Cook," he says with an unintended smile. "Very clannish and vindictive. As I'm sure you know."

"Do you know what happened to your husband?" I ask in a tone that I hope doesn't come off too cautious or guilty.

"He left me, I'm sure," he says breezily. "He said he would if I ever got up to my old tricks. Probably chartered an entire shuttle back to his compound on Knob Hill."

I don't tell him no shuttles could have launched while Mars was still at solar apogee, its farthest point from the sun.

He doesn't seem like a man concerned with the astronomical necessities of travel schedules.

"What about you? Where have you been for two years?" I ask him.

"Here. Half the houses up here are empty. One of them had a little transplant cowl, thus these garish locks. But one has to murder one's time somehow." It was feasible. Most of these homes up here are self-sustaining garrisons of diversion. Self-stocking mini-fridges that aren't so mini. Not to mention skin-jobbing vats. I could have served him at The Church and never known who it was. His problem had never been sustenance. It had been staying dead.

"But why now? Why come to me now?" Harlem II's insistence could hardly have been enough of an incentive.

"I came to warn you. *Caution* you, really. My money has run out. I gave all the credits Rufus allowed me to the Water Builders. They knew about us, about my little dalliance with one of their own and I knew it would be just a matter of time before one or all of them came looking for him. In fact, that was who I thought it was when I noticed you and Carlos slip in that night. I panicked as soon as I heard you two and left through the back door. But I knew they would find me eventually. Start asking questions. So I did what big money does. I sought *them* out and asked their price. I knew I couldn't tell them what had happened to their friend, but I could give them a reason to stop looking. But the automatic credit deposits from Rufus have not been renewed. The Water Builders gave me two years to pay them off. Apparently, a few of them need to go back to Earth to bomb a bison farm in Van Nuys or something. For extortionists, they are very understanding about cash flow issues. But I ran out credits before I paid what we agreed on."

"But that doesn't explain why you're here. I had nothing to do with the death of a Water Builder."

"But Lo did." I swallow in a dry throat when he says this.

"How could they possibly know that?"

"They don't. Not yet. But Harlem II does."

Chapter 41

What did you do with the body on the bed, Carlos, I message frantically after the second Mr. Kant leaves. Traditional text messaging is like sending up smoke signals, an elaborately and comically archaic mode of conveying my fear, but the only thing that ©*Godmother* won't recognize as worthy of modern attention and so won't show up on the group Feed. My iPhone 151 is a quaint little antique I use with Carlos when I'm in a playful mood. My thumbs are rusty and stumble over the keypad.

Why are you texting me? What's next? Gaslight and a music hall revue?

What did you do with it? It's important.

I assume you are referring to that grim little gathering two years ago.

Same.

I did nothing with it. Someone else did the courtesy of removing it for me.

And you know who? There is a two-second lag in his response that seems like an ice age before he answers.

I suspect.

Why did you lie about the DNA test? Why did you tell me it was Kant?

I needed another variable. The boy is still in beta.

Lo might be in danger.

I wish you could hear me sigh, Cook. Isn't it both imminently and appalling clear at this juncture that the boy can take care of himself? Wish the boy a happy Anticipation Day or whatever you're choosing to celebrate. I'm going back to my porn file. Peace. -CY.

Chapter 42

Lo loves his new room. I'm not sure how much a surprise the party is. You could smell the cake cooling all the way to the Syrtis Major Planum. His only concern is for the room's architectural congruity with my farmhouse. I tell him not to worry about it. Having come from Los Angeles, I'm used to schizoid community planning. I'm wary of the Water Builders but I have decided to trust Carlos. I put on my best smile. A stupid party hat Trilla has printed from a vintage Beistle catalogue.

None of the Builds ask with whom I was having tea.

Trilla's made Lo an audio file of pristine days, variations on the Cole Porter Songbook he can play on a small deck built in to a curve above his bed.

I'm right about his tastes.

The bed he chooses is little more than a large clear raindrop of bio-memory gel in a pale green membrane. His commode and shower are efficiently sonic, both a pearly pale pink of smooth curves and recess that a conch might have preferred.

We wait for Lo to "blow" out his "candles," not sure what song to sing. I hum a little Hank Williams instead.

I don't ask what Lo has wished for. What good are wishes for a boy like Lo? We don't plate the cake. We dive into it with our hands. Then we smear it on our faces. Then start throwing what's left of it at each other. We all laugh.

Had Carlos selected for this brand of wasteful playfulness? Or is joy beyond the imposed tenure of a manipulated biological directive?

"Was Harlem II here earlier?" Lo asks when we are alone in his room. I've ©*Godmothere*d my preference to the pale putty that is his couch and wait while it shifts and hardens into the dark tiger-oak sheen of an Arts and Crafts Limbert settle. Lo sits on a bouncy orb that pulses purple and orange. "I could have sworn I heard her laughing this afternoon." He must know the answer to this. Does he just want to hear me say it?

"Yeah. She's safe. Her dad was here, too." This is what he's been waiting for. The look on my face while he observes all the conflicts and computations there. My relief. My fear. My total uncertainty for his safety.

"And you're worried about me. After two years, Cook? Even though the Water Builders have proven to be my friends?" Is that the word he wants to use? *Proven*. One night drifting through the Elysian halls of vegetarian bliss? A cache of strap-on tongues that can barely transmit their full sensory potential with the slop they eat at the yard?

"The Builders are more reasonable than you know, Cook. You just have to give them a chance. Like you've given me a chance. If you want them to act like us, you have to treat them like us. Isn't that what you would say?"

It's not what I would say. I would tell him to forget everything I've said about thinking with his heart when it comes to the Water Builders. I'd tell him to watch his ass.

"I was such a mess after Lily. I thought I was throwing all my craziness at Kant. I'll just tell them I made a mistake. I'll own it, like you say."

But I'm an old man who loves his old music and his old bio-mimetic floors and hand-cranked water pumps. I love the old ways of doing things. And I still have the old Earthbound fears of what really happens to love in the face if intolerance.

The rules are different up here.

Wiloughby is a cold forge that has convinced itself it's hot. So maybe. Just maybe he's right about the Water Builders.

ARBOREAL SUSPENSION AND OTHER ACTS OF LOVE

Chapter 43

I'm not sure there are any real distinctions between student and teacher. I think at any given time, depending on the requirements of circumstance and the receptivity of parties involved, we are all combinations of both.

Working kitchens are not so fluid in their hierarchies. Not nearly so equable. In a kitchen there is only one chef. And I've ever only been a cook.

After Lily's demise graciously inspired Lo's Indian buffet night, that distinction became pretty damn clear. Was it weird working for him? Not really. We basically worked the same only I didn't have to think or worry so much.

Finally sleeping in his own room, he dreamed. And what he dreamed was revelatory.

Goat loin (thawed after two years frozen) stuffed with strawberry chutney and mint, flash fried in its own fat until it had the mouth feel of a meaty churro but rewarded your bite like the most savory jelly donut. Salads of flowering lettuces that looked like bridal bouquets but turned to nutty perfumes at just the touch of a tongue. German chocolate kale flour cakes with vacuum-chamber melted cashew glaze.

Pearl onion and shallot bisque that made a mockery of any memory of the crustacean variety.

Stoner food.

He smashed the tissue printer, literally, our first night back. His eyes had gone wide when pulled his baseball bat away from the mess of memory file scanners and defunct actuators left on the kitchen floor.

"Do you think Carlos will be pissed?" That printer was worth the construction costs of my whole restaurant.

"I think Carlos has already been well compensated. He has a twenty percent take on all The Church's receipts," I smiled.

Culinary expectations on Wiloughby were not hard to supersede.

In the months that had passed, Carlos had allowed population rotations to fill up our tables with all new palates. I never knew if he had lifted his border restrictions because the Build program was over. Or if he just needed the money.

Almost all the palates were new.

The second Mr. Kant and Harlem II were still regulars.

Carlos was so convinced Lo had reached his full potential, that the boy would not perpetrate any new *incidents*, that he even allowed Lo an Earthlink to advertise back home. I have to admit that burned more than a little. My only comfort was in Lo's ever-flowing gratitude. He reminded me nightly, daily, sometimes even in the cool of morning while we picked the night's produce that he could have never done it without me.

That's when *he* became my only signature dish.

The rounded tips of our three Michelin stars where flowers in my crown too, he assured me.

The Church became the destination I had always hoped it would be. Our waiting lists filled, then overflowed, then grew at the queasy download speed of the boy's garden.

Carlos made his contribution, too. He personally contracted for three ship-of-the-line shuttles to be gutted and fitted with feed bays and livestock harness. Even two aquariums, one fresh and one salt. These he had loaded up Old Testament style and shot to our expanded meadow and fishponds. It sounds grander than it was. This was no commercial farm. It still felt sublime and bucolic in my backyard.

Normandy pigs. Cows from Point Rey. Goats from Humboldt County.

We even had two bison from a new farm collective that had sprung up in Van Nuys after one of the owners had found a variety of grass that thrived on sea water. You barely needed to season the meat.

Lo was the perfect animal husband. He controlled population with a whisper, death with a gentle kiss. It sounds like something you might read as a disclaimer at the end of an old John Ford file. But no animals really were ever harmed. When it came time to cull, Lo just massaged them to sleep. Harlem II had even begun to speak, the only problem was she had a habit of walking among the herds of different species, stroking their forelocks and shanks while she giggled names to them.

Then I realized all the ducks were Daisy. All the cows were Maizy. All the goats Hazy. The pigs she named Petunia.

Meat, like everything we served, was only used when available. But it didn't seem to matter. We were still fully committed, even on our vegetarian nights. I looked for the Water Builders on those nights, a gesture of truce that would be their silent bodies seated at a five top, tongues primed in their pouches.

I never knew if Lo had made amends with them. Offered free umami upgrades to their tongues as a sign of truce. I only know they never showed.

It was only after a several of these nights, fruitlessly searching the dining floor for their filthy pale blue jumpsuits, that the reason they didn't show finally became obvious.

They didn't know.

They simply didn't know what had happened to one of their own. They led silent and dangerous lives. Disappearances among their ranks must be fairly commonplace.

Or maybe they were waiting for something.

Chapter 44

The cast concrete ceiling of Carlos Yakamura's bunker is too low for Lo. The boy has grown a full three inches and we'd all been quiet about it, there having never been a similar cramped space or enough rote fatherly attention to put the fact of his height in such stark relief.

I mention how much he's grown as we sit on Carlos Yakamura's candy-colored poofs. My observation seems too self-evident for comment. Only a non-Build would smile shyly or proudly or take credit for something outside of his conscious control.

He's also gotten more handsome, his cheeks and jaw more defined, his nose more aquiline and prominent. His skin is even darker, confirming my suspicions about his confused heritage.

He looks like Carlos Yakamura. I've seen the old photo files of him before he got sick.

Or at least half of Carlos Yakamura.

I don't mention his looks. Not out of a fear that such a comment will meet with another frosty look of self-evidence but because I'm beginning to doubt my assumption that, like the rest of the Builds, Lo's zygote was neutral.

We all come from some place. Or someone. Carlos and Lo discuss the future of The Church. The fiscal complications of expanding the dining room versus the qualitative considerations that would keep it an exclusive dining experience. I listen to their voices.

I hated it the first time I realized I laughed like my father. That low plosive of derision, more nasal than oral, that had shot out of me the day the warden's wife brought me the only letter I would ever receive while I was in jail. It had been a letter from my father, a yellowed, retro looking card with a picture of a freaked-out kitten clinging to the end of a rope by a single tiny claw. "Hang In There, Baby," the caption read.

He had signed it "D."

Just "D." I remember running the uncommitted initial through the filter of my feelings for him as I sat on my cot, looking at his card.

Dipshit.

Doper.

Dumbfuck.

Denialist.

I couldn't stop the letter from informing my feelings about my mother as well.

Distanced.

Dishonored.

Dead.

Then the letter had worked its litanies on me.

Dolorous.

Desperate.

Disenchanted.

Dumb.

I wonder if Lo hears it, the same grunts of approval, the way they both downplay their intellectual fluency by mumbling technical jargon. The studied lockstep of his speaking cadence that he clearly shares with the fox. They both even pull their faces back the same way with their hands when they listen to the other speak.

If my suspicions about their relation is true, Carlos must have been a very charismatic if enticingly remote man before his illness.

What's it like for him to sit with a perfected version of himself? Is he proud of his work, of the safeguard for the future the boy is becoming? Or has the real motivation for creating Lo just been raw vanity after all? I'm so enthralled with my thoughts I don't hear that the conversation has stopped on both fronts.

"You still with us, Cook?" the fox asks. "Do you think we could work a kickback deal with the shuttle companies that would offset potential losses from not expanding?" Lo is quick in his repost.

"Or do you think we could open a shop on Earth and turn The Church into more of a test kitchen?" I'm quick in my response, too.

"You're going to sacrifice quality if you make The Church anything but a destination experience. But if you tack on the deferred cost of a kickback, you'll inflate the cover price past consistent capacity."

They regard me in silence, but I can't think why. The answer is obvious.

Isn't that the whole point of Wiloughby? That it's *not* racked with the lifestyle limits and corporate motivations of Earth?

"I think you should just leave The Church alone. And start counting your blessings." They finally sit back in their seats, odd reflections of one another and seem satisfied with my answer. I'm just glad I can still earn my keep.

Carlos uncoils from his seat on the floor to get up and make tea. Lo looks at me sheepishly.

"I can't believe the conversation went there. I don't know what I was thinking."

"You're thinking you've got a hit on your hands," I say to him. "It's normal to want to exploit that."

I had closed The Cage at the Calabasas Correctional Center one week after my first sterling reviews. I just wasn't angry anymore. At least that's what I told myself at the time. The warden had floated the idea of commuting my sentence to community service if I'd agree to manning the grill at a new shop on Sunset. He said he had backers that were interested in resurrecting the old Nancy Silverton brand and I could umbrella my talents under the Chi Spacca reboot.

The truth is, I was afraid to leave jail.

I thought that if I did my father would finally have a reasonable excuse to not come back for me.

The Cage wasn't first principal cooking, anyway. It was a gimmick, a fuck you to the monied gullets who shared stock portfolios and Super Bowl box seats with families just like mine. Lo had created something entirely different. Something real and worth protecting. But more importantly, something worth *trusting*. Every cook knows they're only at their best when being of service to something more diverse, more complex, and far more flavorful than themselves.

"You've got to remember why you're doing it, Lo. Why you strap an apron on every day."

"You're right."

I was sick of being right.

Sick of hearing myself.

Sick of my meager and redundant "atta boys."

The kid didn't need confirmation. Or guidance. He just needed to trust himself.

And I needed to let him.

I don't know where I was thinking of going. Back to the farmhouse to see if the animals needed their water troughs filled. Back to the garden where maybe little Harlem II was waiting for me to continue my catechism on bees. She had been fascinated by the idea of insect pollination, an idea that had the dubious ring of a fairy-tale here on Wiloughby. I'd called the drones "preacher bees" and she had feigned shock at the indecent way we "consummated" our plants by hand.

"You mean they're not really *married,* Cook," she'd said, wide-eyed and in a way that had turned my heart to simple syrup.

"We have no bees on Wiloughby, honey. All the flower marriages up here are common law."

"That's *awful*."

Or maybe I'd just head back to Earth and do what every cook did who saw the curtain closing on the second act of their careers. Lease the requisite food truck that doled out the requisite fried and over-sweetened comfort food that late-night stoners and Bel Air slummers could only "find" via my requisitely cryptic ©*Godmother* bings. Or I could get really "edgy" and charter a delivery drone service that made drops from a gentrified soup kitchen on Sixth Street. My options, as were their habit, were becoming increasingly less interesting.

Then the lid on the teapot that Carlos had just placed on his coffee table begins to rattle. The fox's eyes narrow. Lo opens his mouth to speak but the sound of a massive concussion above us stops him.

"What the hell was that?"

"Was that an *explosion*?"

We are thrown to the floor by the shockwave. Concrete dust rains down on Carlos's Caucasian rugs. Lo and I watch helplessly while Carlos, calm as a canine bodhisattva closes his eyes to ©*Godmother* a link to Wiloughby's civic systems mainframe.

"The oxygen mix tanks at the Water Builder's yard just exploded," he says in a soft voice, like he was reciting a *zen koan* on total destruction.

"*What's* happening?"

But before Carlos can answer we hear the sound of a distant hiss. "Dark noise" the cosmologists call it, the deep and steady pneumatic leaking of the universe. But this sound could not soothe you to sleep like it had countless astronomers who have fallen asleep in the seats of their massive telescopes, earbuds still clinging to the shells of their ears.

This sound gets louder, builds in volume until it shakes Carlos' bunker like a stadium crowd cheering for an encore in a hurricane.

"That would be the anti-combustion default kicking in," Carlos says, looking up at his ceiling. It has formed at least one large dark spot of moisture.

"The what?" I ask.

"The sound, Cook, of ten point nine billion gallons of perfectly rendered water gushing from their relief valves and flooding with a projected saturation level of one-cubic meter all of the arable land in a two-mile circumference of Wiloughby."

"Are the mix tanks on *fire*, Carlos?" Lo asks, far more calmly than I could manage.

"Nothing is on fire, guys," Carlos says evenly, opening his eyes. "Not for more than a second anyway. How ever this happened, whomever is responsible, did not want Wiloughby to burn. They wanted to *flood* it."

I'm speechless.

I can't get my mind to jump over what I've just heard, can't bridge the gap between my very recent thoughts about culinary integrity and little girls obsessed with bees and stupid food trucks and the very real but still entirely inconceivable thought that the Wiloughby we knew is no longer above us.

"But that's not the worst part," the fox says, not breaking a sweat even if he could. I laugh with that hideous dad-inspired nasal laugh.

"It's not?"

"No. Wiloughby's electrical systems are wirelessly transmitted but the generator is powered by cold fusion. If water finds its way down into the reactor core, collateral damage will be the least of our worries."

End-of-the-world scenarios are for antiquated VR games, mid-late twentieth-century disaster film files.

It's not what a staggering genius canned in a mechanical fox discusses with two cooks, one in obvious ascent, the other begrudgingly eyeing the exit.

But it's what's happening.

Or happened.

Or is in the very real and super fucking terrifying process of *about* to happen.

Carlos is not very clear.

He shows no signs of being outwardly alarmed. In fact, he is infuriatingly in no hurry at all. Why should he be? Carlos had already died once. The little shit doesn't even need to take a breath unless it's to punctuate a point he's making.

I want to know what might have caused it.

"Don't you mean *who?*" Carlos smirks.

Water Builders.

Patient bastards.

He knows the Water Builders are responsible. He knows the oxygen mix tanks are guarded by over fifteen safety protocols and defaults, all of which would have taken weeks to dismantle, all of which would *have* to have been overridden manually. He even knows *why* they did it. All three of us do. That makes all three us guilty for what has happened.

Two by omission. The other by virtue of his run-away hormones.

We know now, for sure, the Water Builders did *not* know who was directly and indirectly responsible for the killing of one of their own. If they had known, only one or all three of us would be dead at this moment.

Not *all* of Wiloughby.

I wonder if this is what Carlos had meant when he had texted me about adding another variable to the mix.

He says there is a possibility that someone or thing could have survived. He tells us this only after he gives us a small lecture on the tertiary adaptive strategy that evolution, or modified descent, as he is fonder of saying, had imposed on creatures who had developed the capacity to breath a corrosive and flammable gas like oxygen.

Like I said, the fox is not in a hurry.

The "wind of fire," which is what he calls the explosion on Wiloughby, savoring the biblical implications of the term, is what it sounds like. The breathable air, for just a flashing instant, had been ignited. That would be a major complication for every creature on Wiloughby. Everyone but Carlos.

"So if anyone or anything was *breathing*, they'd be dead?" I ask to be clear.

"No. If anyone or thing was breathing *in*? Yes. Most likely their lungs would have caught fire with the oxygen they were letting into their bodies," the fox explains. "But exhaling? Not so much. The CO2 would have formed a buffer. You have to understand the conflagration we heard lasted a mere *second* before the anti-combustion protocols kicked in."

"Only a second?" Lo says. "It felt longer." It is the first and only time he has spoken in what feels like long and hideous hours.

"I'm just curious about the nuclear core thing you mentioned," I say, barely containing my frustration. "The fact that it might go critical if water gets on it or whatever. I'm just trying to reconcile that with your pretty laid-back attitude."

"I'm keeping track of the time, Cook. Don't worry," the fox says either ignoring or dismissing my sarcasm. "I simply have to wait for the hollows of the containment tanks that *surround* the core to flood so the water can hopefully cool the access hatch."

The *cold* in cold fusion must be a relative term.

"Someone has to *swim* down there to shut the thing off?" Lo asks.

"Right. Shunt the power feedback that keeps the core sparked so we can reset it and get it back online after we drain it."

"What's this reset look like?" I ask. "Is it a switch? A lever? A kind of *toggle*?"

"I'll do it," Lo speaks up for the third time. "No offense, Cook, but it's kind of a combination of all those things including a six—"

"Seven—" Carlos corrects.

"*Seven*-digit code. Only one problem," the boy says with a shy grin. "I can't swim."

"Lo, you don't have to do this," I say.

"Yes, I do," he says simply, factually. Hadn't I been the one to tell him, however lamely, that actions or, in his case, uncontrolled *feelings,* have consequences?

Shelley Winters, I think to myself. The first *Poseidon Adventure,* not the crappy remake or sequel. This is precisely what I was talking about when I mentioned the provenance of our current situation. Strictly B-movie double bill fodder.

Then why aren't I laughing in that paternal way I hate?

"You can't do all this *remotely,* Carlos?" I ask, seeming to be the only one who recognizes blind panic as a reasonable response to our situation.

"No, Cook. That's why we *have* Water Builders," he says, sipping his tea. "I just never thought I'd be indirectly responsible for pissing them off."

Chapter 45

I've gotten my casting wrong.

Lo isn't Shelley Winters in our scenario. I am. I'm the old one hunched over a comfortable gut who's neglected his endorphin upgrades along with the gym. Swimming won't be a problem for Lo just as long as *I* know how to swim, the fox informs me.

This makes sense on Wiloughby.

Before Lo cultivated the garden that gave The Church its new direction, he wandered through another garden.

This garden had been closed to him or offered to him, depending on your position on private gardens.

I mean the garden of my mind. My memories.

Like most gardens of this nature, it was largely unattended. Overgrown with forbidden briars and once-flowering plants that had since turned to tall and neglected weeds. He wandered it freely, plucking what was of interest to him (my basic convictions about cooking, the color and nutritive texture of certain Los Angeles lawns, lonely mammoths suffering from thousands of years of historical displacement and poor air conditioning) discarding to the loamy ground that which wasn't of interest (most of my fatherly advice).

His harvesting of this garden was the most-gentle of larcenies. He didn't know he was stealing from me.

But this time would be different. This time, with the help of Carlos and a comfortable rug, I would invite him in. Let him cut from me an entire bouquet of what arms and legs and faces do when they want to move in water.

Lo is not in the bunker with us. He braved the gush of water that fell on him when he opened the submarine hatch of Carlos' bunker and crept out into whatever Wiloughby has become. I can't see what he's seeing. Can't hear what he's hearing. Not yet.

Carlos tells me to lay back into the thick nap of his rug and relax. Focus on my breathing.

Not the million gallons of water that might be eating their way toward the reactor core. Not on the well-being of the people out of focus above me. Or our precious livestock. Or the fact that our vegetable beds are now struggling not to become pond growth.

Fear locks the mind.

I have to open mine.

Open my mind and "offer" swimming. Not the memory or technique of it. All of that is deep in my autonomic nervous system now, pure instinct for me.

I have to *be* swimming.

I am talking of a summer on Zuma Beach in Malibu, at the white confluence of sound absorbing sand that muddles with the shore near Paradise Cove. The soft machine of the tides lapping and retracting at my toes that hot late

August day when I am now so convincingly disguised as a six-year-old boy.

It's been almost a year since my mother has "fitted" me with her beta version of the ©*Pumpkin.* My sinus still itches. My dreams are not my own. My dad has brought me here because even ©*Godmother* is quieted by the surf. The heat is oppressive and delicious. I can hear myself sweat.

I've been making drip castles, spraying them from a little bottle of polymer coating I've brought so they will harden and I can bring the best of them home. I watch my dad in the breakers as he learns to surf on the new sliver boards, agile planks of hand-shaped soy foam no bigger than a snow ski.

He's good at anything physical.

I smile when he catches a wave and slices through the tube without a single cutback. He rides it to the shore, slowing over the holes in the wet sand the sand crabs make when they come up for air. I wish he would wave me over, help me paddle out past the chop and teach me how to use it. But he's back in the soup, leaping like a Labrador pup over the breakers, not seeing me.

Or pretending not to.

The water is cold on my skin and welcome. This is back when the ocean was purely recreational, before the huge snouts of the de-salination pumps raised the temperature of the brine to lukewarm dish water. I squat through a small wave, getting my body used to the cold before I push off from the bottom and frog stroke into the swell. The lights on the automated life-guard kiosk glow green.

It's a perfect day for swimming.

I remember doing a dead-man's float that day, face down in the drink, eyes open and stinging as they tried to focus on the murky bottom.

But this version of that day is different.

Something tells me to paddle out to the swim-line that bobs between the shallows and where the bottom falls sharply beneath the deep water. I feel the joints of my shoulders and thighs engage and I am pulling myself easily through the light chop. Face down then rotated laterally for a breath. Pulling and pulling with no resistance, the liquid salt sheeting off me as if I were a baby seal. I don't remember ever having swum with my eyes closed.

But this day is different. I slow into a dog paddle, shaking the wet from my hair and open my eyes.

These are not my eyes I'm seeing through.

This is not the taste of my breath.

Or what I know to be the familiar rush of my blood. What I see is *not* the Malibu shore.

It is Wiloughby. Or what is left of it.

I panic. I cough water out of my lungs. I hear Carlos' calm voice whisper to me from the shore.

Easy, Cook. You're inside Lo's head now. Just observe it and keep swimming.

I breaststroke easily through the fresh-water river that is now Wiloughby's main street. Speckle-back trout dart silver and fleet beneath my belly. At least The Church's stock of fresh-water fish has survived.

The houses have not faired so well.

They are black at the cornices and sills where the flash fire has toasted them. The water is head high at all their locked doors.

A still corked magnum of Cristal champagne bobs without a message past my shoulder. An open laptop, the screen still blue and cursor flashing, waiting for a prompt. A chartreuse Chanel gown undulates underwater like a drowned ghost at the partially submerged gate of the Kant's house. The bloated corpse of one of our pigs drifts past me, waxy and pale. An Alaskan salmon nibbles at the bristles on its haunch.

I don't feel horror or remorse. These eyes I'm borrowing don't acknowledge such emotions. In fact, it's surprisingly calm in Lo's head.

Lo is enjoying his feeling of weightlessness, of riding in the skiff of his own body while I pull the oars.

The purple grass of the Water Builder's yard beneath me sways gracefully like pond cress, like the first Harlem's hair the one time I saw her dance. Debris from the exploded mix tank is everywhere, some as small as floating shrapnel. Others as big as an old airplane fuselage. Shards of sunken wreckage are tangled in the grass along with one of the Water Builder's tongues, the taste cognition wires drifting in the shallow current like the tendrils of a dead jellyfish.

There's no shock when I see the bobbing corpse of the first Water Builder.

No sense of relief when I see the second one.

I'm only allowed a remote melancholy, more happy than sad when I recognize the cropped blonde head of the

Builder girl who once hugged Lo. She had really enjoyed her vegetarian meal at The Church that night.

The reactor is larger than I imagined, rising up twenty feet above my head out of the water that laps lazily at its circular walls. The door to the shell is blocked by the pressure of the water but there is another way in.

A gantry of criss-crossed metal at the reactor's base that acted as a cooling vent.

I have to dive to the base to inspect it.

Most of the vent's huge mesh is intact, allowing for an egress of only a few square centimeters. But around the back of the vent the impact of the explosion has loosened a section that I can pry apart and fit inside. I am frustrated when I realize Lo's thin arms can't budge it. I see air bubbles escape before his eyes. I want him to stop. Surface. Take another breath. But the determination I feel brimming inside him won't let him. I see his fingers lace through the mesh of the vent, the knuckles turning white with the effort. Nothing. I feel him somersault into his back like an Olympic swimmer kick-turning for another lap. He kicks at the vent with both feet. The vent finally gives. More air bubbles glitter past his eyes. *Surface. Surface.* I feel his lungs scream for oxygen as he dives back down into the hole in the vent. I can see the core reset controls submerged in another twenty feet of flood water beneath me. I swim back out for a breath.

"I need him to stop, Carlos," I sputter. "It's too deep. He won't make it."

"There's no limbic synthesis with the neural link, Cook," the fox says calmly. "He can't feel what you feel."

I'm just a passenger in the car of Lo's mind. I watch helplessly as he configures his next move. He's going to need some ballast if he's going to stay down there long enough to reset the reactor core. He swims among the wreckage of the holding tanks, testing chunks and shards for weight. He finds a few pieces that might serve him and stuffs them into the bib of his overalls. He starts dog paddling furiously as he begins to sink.

One deep breath. That's all I feel him take. He freefalls down into the depths near the control panel.

Something is wrong.

I don't know why I haven't felt it.

I only see the inky trail of his blood as it seeps like smoke from his side. He must have cut himself when he stuffed the shrapnel into his clothes. I don't know how deep his cut is. He doesn't seem too concerned. He's too busy enjoying his languid freefall to the reset controls.

I don't focus on what his hands do once he's down there, his confident fingers that check the integrity of the reactor door.

I only see the thin reddish curls of what's leaking from him where the ballast has cut him. His movements are precise as he enters the seven-digit reset code. His final task. He yanks the ballast from his clothes to resurface. Has he cut himself deeper? Or is the change in pressure as he rises making his blood flow quicker?

Turner's grand storms.

Rothko's citrusy gradients.

I don't feel the pressure screaming in his lungs anymore. Or the flush of euphoria that's gaining traction in his dimming brain. I can only inform the oars of his arms. The paddles of his feet. But his arms and feet are no longer moving. The only thing moving before his eyes is the reddening of the water around him.

I sputter awake, puking water onto Carlos' floor.

"Did you get him to the surface, Cook?" the fox asks fearfully. "*Did* you?" I can feel my head loll on the rug, but I can't clear it. "Cook! Cook, look at me!"

I feel the fox's tiny claws rake my face, stinging and drawing some of my own blood. "Cook! Cook, wake *up!*"

I'm miles from the Malibu shore, the heat of the California sun and brackish surf slowing my strokes, weighting me, pulling me downward.

Chapter 46

"You know Shelley Winters was a competitive swimmer, before her first contract with Warner," the fox informs me. Carlos is clinging to my back as I frog stroke my second time down Wiloughby's flooded main street. "She might have been the new Esther Williams if she'd been born earlier."

He's telling me this to distract me, to keep my mind off the radiant horror that's bleaching my mind at what I see all around me. "She did her own stunts in *The Poseidon Adventure.* Not many people know that."

He doesn't need to distract me. The chalky taste of the adrenaline mint he'd stuck in my mouth to revive me is distracting enough.

Chapter 47

The Martian soil has a deep memory of water. The massive dry canals on her surface attest to this.

The water had begun to recede.

And even as I'm swimming, as we approach the Water Builders yard, as I feel my knees begin to graze the gravel on the soggy paths, I realize this red planet has known all along what to do with water.

The purple grass is deflated, just yards of dead dark hair heaped upon itself. The lifeless bodies of the five remaining Water Builders are strewn everywhere on the slumbering grass, battlefield style. I think of those old Brady photographic files of Shiloh. Gettysburg. There are even animals strewn about, stiffened and hoofed.

But they are not horses.

We find Lo face down by the now-waterless gantry at the reactor's base. I turn him over.

His wound still seeps.

"You know we couldn't have waited for the water to recede, Cook," the fox says, climbing to the soggy ground from my back. "This was the only way."

I drop to my knees to touch him. His skin is cold and clammy. I can't feel a pulse.

I brush the hair back from his face while my whole heart falls and the hot tears rise up in my eyes.

"Lo?" I say patting his face. "Lo, can you hear me?" I push my ear to his chest. Tip his head back as his jaw falls open. I blow into his cold mouth.

"Is he dead?"

"Get the water out of his lungs," the fox says, as he holds up a single claw. I push on his chest. Water gushes past his lips.

"What are you going to do?"

The fox touches Lo on the meat of his limp shoulder.

"Is he dead? What did you just do?"

The fox just stares at me, stony as the toy he resembles.

"You think you can manage carrying him by yourself back to my burrow?" Carlos says finally.

Oh, Cook. I say to myself. How many times do you have to hear it repeated?

When will you shed that worn out Earthbound morality of yours?

Don't you know nothing ever really dies on Wiloughby?

Chapter 48

Don't ask me to explain it.

I don't even try to understand Carlos's tinkering with the boy's body.

He has him neck deep in the mouth of some iron lung-looking thing that buzzes like a cheaply printed vibrator some Rodeo Drive trophy wife might have whipped up to pass another lonely Beverly Hills night. Carlos says he's vacuumed his lungs, injected him with nano t-cells to repair what damage he can.

But this black magic is a poor kind of sorcery.

The fox informs me the boy's wounds are mortal. He's just lost too much blood, gone too long without oxygen. The tin sleeping bag he's tucked into is supposed to keep him comfortable, revive him just long enough for Carlos to sequence his DNA for reconstitution.

I insist Carlos make no changes in him. I want the boy exactly as he was.

"You won't have long with him, Cook," Carlos says, as he punches a few buttons on the iron lung. "Maybe just a couple of hours."

Lo just looks sleepy when he comes to, like a little boy trying to keep his eyes open at his first late night drive-in movie. Or am I talking about myself?

His voice is raspy and weak when he speaks.

"Hey, Cook. What did I miss?" I don't bother to wipe my eyes or steady my voice when I repeat myself.

"I was just saying we can start over right where we left off. Carlos has a zygote all ready to go and this time I can raise you myself. From scratch. You'll still be Carlos' son. But *my* little boy this time. My *son*. You can show me how to plant a whole new garden, how to cook like you do. And I'll listen. I'll help. Like we used to only better this time. We can re-open The Church if you want. Call it something else. The First Principal Cafe. Or is that too corny."

The boy smiles but he has already made up his mind.

"No, Cook," he says thinly. "Not this time. I don't want to be me again. Not even a better version of me. It's too hard. It's just too hard."

I don't want to hear this.

Can't bear to hear this.

"No. You *have* to come back," I say, squeezing his weak hand. "You *learned*. You can learn again. The hard part's over."

He silences me with a slow shake of his head.

"Come here," he whispers. "It's too much to talk like this."

I lean down into him.

What he whispers to me makes my whole body wrack with sobs. Makes me smile through my tears.

I don't recognize my farmhouse when I come upon it later that day. It looks like something the Post-Modernist artist Cristo would have spent a fortune wrapping in thick rubbery gauze. Lo is breathing slowly in the suspension gurney that hovers beside me. I want him to wake up and see it. See our house one last time.

It takes me a moment to realize what's happened.

Lo's room of living walls has expanded to hug my entire house, protect it from the fire and flood that has devastated most of Wiloughby. I look up at the gently throbbing coating that towers two stories above me. It is warm when I touch it, rippling like I've tickled it. Then the coating slowly starts to recede. A cotton sheet pulled from the dustless shine on an old piano. A great albino python as it coils gently back into its original shape of a snail that is Lo's new old room.

My farmhouse is exactly as I'd left it. The studied cant of my roofline. The imposed sag in my front porch. I'm guilty at my good fortune. I push Lo up my front steps and lay him down in his old hickory rocker. Like he asked me to when he whispered to me. He folds into it, his legs too weak to find their old perch at the rim of the seat.

"You all right?"

"Just go put on some of that horrible Hank Williams," he smiles to me. "Then go upstairs, Cook. I don't want you to watch me do it."

I don't like it.

I want to stay here with him.

But he's past saying anything else.

I watch him through the screen door. My view through the mesh has already made him begin to fade.

I head up the stairs, propelled perhaps by the familiar creak of the treads that has always mocked the end of my day. On the landing, closing my bedroom door is Isaac. Harlem II sleeps soundly in his arms. He hugs me with one arm while he cradles Harlem with the other. We don't say anything.

We have all the time in the world for that.

He opens my bedroom door to show me Trilla laying on my bed.

"She went out to play a scalding desert day when she heard the water start coming. A variation on Brahms Requiem, second movement," he says slowly, still stunned. "I tried to stop her, but Harlem started wailing. She was up to the vocal section when the flood took her. I only found her body this morning. I don't know what happened to her keyboard." I take the baby while he drops to his knees.

Speaking it has made it real for him. I watch him weep while Harlem squirms in my arms.

She wants me to put her down. She wants to go to the weeping Build. I let her. She wraps her tiny arms around Isaac as he smiles. He knows his tears are temporary. He knows the odd Eskimo logic, that isolated native magic that reigns here on Wiloughby.

We will both see Trilla again.

Chapter 49

The next morning the sunlight is weak as it filters through the window in my bedroom. Shaded, somehow shrouded. I would think Trilla had composed a gloomy day to go with our mood, a variation on "A Foggy Day in London Town."

But I know better.

It's early when I creep down my stairs. The baby still sleeps, curled into Isaac who breaths evenly on my front room couch. I head into my kitchen to boil water for coffee. Looking out my kitchen window I see what's left of our garden. Red rusty puddles stain the wilted crops. A pair of wire-haired hogs rout in the bloody mud of the potato patch. It should feel like the end of something. But I know it is just the beginning.

I step out onto my porch and look up.

The tree is massive, far bigger than Lo led me to believe it would be.

I am neither, Lo had once said to me. *I am the rectory tree. And the tree does not need to decide.*

It has woven its thick roots through his hickory rocking chair bursting through the planks of my front porch where it has found ample moisture in the dark earth beneath the porch's support posts. The canopy of the tree has broken through the roof of my porch, unfurling in all directions. It throws a welcome shade through the front windows of both stories. The branches are massive tangles of dark rippling bark that taper to rich leafy runners that have already begun to flower.

Perfect for climbing. Or hanging a chain swing for summer evenings. I recognize the flowers from their various shapes and smell. Pink grapefruit and Macintosh apple blossom. Cara Cara orange and sweet avocado. The skirt of pinot grape leaves at the base of the trunk makes me smile. It's what he'd promised. It will live and give forever.

I am the rectory tree and the tree does not have to decide.

WILOUGHBY AND ALMOST EVERYTHING AFTER

Chapter 50

Little Trilla, *new* Trilla, likes ragtime, so the days are always playful and sunny. I worry about breaking her little heart, but I need some rain if this new crop is going to make it to harvest before we re-open The Church.

I'm going full vegetarian now. No more culling. I've had enough blood.

Just a little flock of goats graze in the meadow. I'm becoming known back on Earth for the soft funk of my unpasteurized chevre.

The flood water let the roots of Lo's original garden run deep. The portrait planted there is still me, but a different me. Older and sadder if you judge by the way the carrot tops fringe the new bulbs of Japanese pumpkins that make the eyes.

Or maybe it's the bees.

Harlem II two has fallen in love with bugs, but still favors the bees. She loves to take me to her bee houses that she's set up in front of Lo's old room where she lives. She uses no smoker when she harvests their honey.

No gloves or mesh on her sun hat to protect herself from their stings.

Her drones know who is the real queen of their hives.

She is teaching her bees to write but she is having trouble teaching them their words in English. She pulls out a screen as her honey-makers respectfully depart and shows me the sweet syrupy geometric wax of their home.

There are letters there.

INYECNKINYANKE, the tiny dripping octagons seem to spell out in the dark solids where the new drones are hatching.

"What's it mean?" I ask, fascinated.

"Minus the phonetic ligatures it translates from Lakota into "'It Stares,'" she says.

She has just turned four.

I don't get it.

She huffs in mock exasperation. "Don't you understand, Cook? These bees come from the North region of The First Nations Federation back on Earth. What you used to call North Dakota." She explains how they were rescued from the chassis of a '48 Ford on the old Rosebud reservation before the unified tribal council reinstated its sovereignty. The bees had set up a hive in one of the headlights. "When colonized Lakota first saw cars, they saw the old round headlights and thought they looked like eyes. 'It Stares'," she says proudly from her height of one meter. "You get it now?"

I got it.

"It's all they can seem to write. I guess they're just not used to Wiloughby yet."

"Maybe the bees are talking about you. You stare at them enough." She crosses her arms over her chest, throwing back her little head defiantly as she thinks. Her feet are splayed in a perfect first position. She has some of the first Harlem in her.

"Possibly. Now if I could only teach them *English,*" she muses.

"Maybe *you* should learn Lakota."

Her small head drops thoughtfully to her small shoulder. It's a common gesture with her, at once epiphanic and adorable. I pat the back of her head as she scampers to the base of the massive fruiting tree that grows from my front porch. Its bark is rubbed and shiny in spots where her small hands, knees, and feet have climbed it.

It's a favorite spot of hers to think, to study.

I watch her pick a hard red apple from a branch, a soft white peach from another, before she curls herself into the crotch of the main trunk.

She'll need the blood sugar, the rocket fuel, if she's going to launch her intention all the way to the blue haze just above Earth when she hacks into the Feed's Indigenous Languages data base.

I encourage her curiosity, like I do with all the Builds that live with me.

But her effort might prove purely academic.

She's still too small to climb up to the top branches of the tree.

But I climb up there all the time.

From up there you can see where my original meadow has spread all the way to the horizon. The new crop of Isaac's living houses is coming in nicely, the paths between them green with low turf and flowering weeds. People come to Wiloughby now because it is so green. Some to remember green. Others to see it for the first time.

It's nice to see Wiloughby from up here, the low hills rolling into the sky where the purple grass and the mix tanks of the Builder's yard once grew.

We don't build water up here anymore.

We've found our way back to first principals.

At least until our new Trilla matures into her full meteorological repertoire.

When the days get too dry, we soothe the heart of our rain-wisher's sky with Trilla's old recording of her wettest days.

Variations on Eric Satie.

Isaac has buried speakers sporadically through the red hills. It's beautiful to watch from up there. The way the music, muted through the soil, begins to rise up and congeal into finger-like vibrations that drift and curl into the dark knots of gathering clouds before those knots are slowly undone and the clouds become darker and the rain comes down as softly as a lover's hair before bed.

The view is busy up in the tree's canopy, stirred as it is by hundreds of buzzing flight trails. Some of Harlem II's rogue bees have refused to commute from her apiaries and have moved into a knothole up here. These are expeditious bees, thrifty bees, bees that don't see the point of living far away from the flowering currency the tree provides them.

Lo would have approved of these bees, welcomed, I think, being inhabited by them.

I know I welcome them.

And not for their honey and loud company.

I miss Lo. Even though I see him every day. I know he is with me every time I pull a pear tart out of my enclave or lay up a batch of cardamon spiced apple butter. Or mash one of his avocados into spicy guac to go over my zucchini chip nachos.

All that is evidence of him. I miss the first principal of him, the day to day of him.

I miss talking to him.

Perhaps Harlem II's attempt at teaching her hive English has not gone unrewarded.

The knothole up here in the tallest branches of the boy that is now a tree is clotted with a caul of sweet honeycomb.

Peach flower, if I'm not mistaken.

To the bees it is a home. To me it is a kind of organic computer screen. At least I hope it is. I don't tell Harlem II my hope. I need to keep it to myself. Until I'm sure.

Just the other night I came up here. I was missing him. It was the fourth anniversary of the Wiloughby Flood after all. So I did what I had seen the boy once do the day he first planted seeds in what was to be my garden portrait.

I talked to the tree.

I had so much to say, so much news to share. I didn't know where to start. So I had just said "hello."

The next day there was a message for me in the dark pixels of the honeycomb. A brief message, or so I thought at first. Just two letters.

The boy has a name. The boy's name is Lo.

LO the honeycomb had spelled out. The letters pulsed with the murky movements of the young bees dancing in their nurseries that wrote them.

Just like the world's first message on what would one day become the Feed had pulsed when that first transmission failed and inspired the boy's name.

But the bees were still learning.

They were still working.

And like that first transmission, the message was slow in coming.

But this time it would not fail.

The next evening the LO had turned into LLO.

Today it happened. Today the honeycomb read HELLO COOK.

The bees or what was whispering to them was coming through.

About the Author

Bradford Tatum has worked as an actor and writer in both film and television. He lives in Los Angeles with his wife and daughter. His first novel, *Only the Dead Know Burbank* was published by HarperCollins in 2016.

Connect with Bradford and download a free copy of his eBook, I Can Only Give You Everything at BradfordTatum.com/giveaway.

Made in the USA
Las Vegas, NV
20 November 2022

59893485R00184